Icing

The Icing

EMILY MAY

NEWMAN SPRINGS PUBLISHING
320 Broad Street
Red Bank, NJ 07701

First originally published by Newman Springs Publishing 2023

ISBN 979-8-88763-327-5 (Paperback)
ISBN 979-8-88763-328-2 (Digital)

Printed in the United States of America

To Mom and Dad for the confidence to do anything
and Regina Husband, for a Christmas miracle
that allowed me to finish this book.

Sunny

Jake has that look in his eye, the one that tells me when he is up to something. I don't know if I can take any more excitement today. I have something I need to share with him, but I think I will wait until after tonight's looming event. He is deep in thought as his gaze has me frozen and mesmerized while we sit on the island in the middle of the kitchen. I feel my cheeks turn red as my skin starts to tingle with carnal desire. I break his sensual stare and continue to play with my eggs.

"I love that I can still make my beautiful wife blush," Jake boasts, shoveling the rest of his pancakes in his mouth. He stands up, plate in hand, and pushes the stool back with his foot. He makes his way over to me before he throws his dishes in the sink and kisses my head sweetly.

"What time are we leaving for the reunion?" I question as my stomach tightens and my throat becomes dry. Jake heads toward me. His eyes are soft and loving. I put my fork down and shift on the stool so I can face the love of my life.

"We will have fun tonight," he promises.

His hand is soft under my chin as I look up at him. I stand, pushing the chair behind me.

The floor is cool beneath my feet. Jake pulls me in close, and his hands caress my back as they make their way down my backside. I lean against him, finding comfort with my head buried in his chest. His warmth surrounds me as nothing else can. I feel his fingers tug at the hem of my nightgown.

"Lift your arms, beautiful," he instructs as he takes a step back, leaving some space between us.

I obey Jake and lift my arms. Sliding the silk from my body, he licks his lips, and I watch his thirst take over his body. My body is covered with goose bumps as he tosses my nightgown on the floor and stares at me while I stand naked in front of him.

I will never deny my appetite for my husband. I was attracted to him the second I saw him, and I knew I wanted to be with him for the rest of my life. Jake is a few years older than me and grew up in the city, about twenty minutes away. It wasn't until a few months after I graduated that we met. I had scheduled and paid for an art retreat, a small graduation gift to myself, but the night before I left, I was overly depressed. If it weren't for my parents encouraging me to go, I would never have met Jake.

Once at the retreat, I began unpacking my things for the weekend. I looked out the window, and at the same time, his big brown doe eyes caught my gaze. I must have captured his eye as well because he waited for me outside the cottage door until I came out to go to orientation. He introduced himself as Jake Thompson. He went on to explain that he was not an artist, just an ADA. But his boss talked him into taking some time to destress after Jake won a big case. We have been together ever since that day. We didn't wait long to get married. Jake proposed six months after we met, and we were married a year after that.

Holding my hands, he guides my arms down, stopping about halfway. He takes a step back. His jaw tightens as he looks me up and down. "Stunning," he whispers. I smile and drop my head like I always do when I'm embarrassed.

Do I tell him now, or should I let him enjoy himself? I decide to keep my secret until after we get home. It will give me something to focus on tonight—something to look forward to.

Dropping my arms, he pulls me securely against his body. I feel safe for now; later is another story. The butterflies are stirring already.

"I have something for you upstairs." He must feel my cheeks round as I can't help but let my imagination run dirty. "Not that, my sweet girl." He seems amused. "I mean, I can give that to you too, but it's not as pretty as what I got you," he says, kissing the top of my head.

"I love your surprises."

"Good. After you." He lets go of me and stands aside.

"May I have my nightgown back?"

"No, you may not. I can't let something so beautiful be covered by anything so long as the beautiful thing is in this house."

"Oh, are we playing games now?" I tease, walking past him, making sure to sway my hips a little more than usual. Jake brings out pieces of myself I never knew existed.

I can feel the heat from his body close behind me as we walk past the picture windows that are barely covered. Starting up the stairs, my skin prickles as Jake caresses my bottom with the tips of his fingers. By the time we reach the landing, his fingers are inside of me. I take a few steps down the hall and then stop.

As I turn toward him, he is waiting and swallows my mouth with his. He pushes me against the wall. He lifts me, and I wrap my legs around him. He pushes into me and slams me into the wall, knocking down one of my original paintings. Neither of us gives it any thought as it hits the floor hard, and we continue to enjoy each other. I can feel his breath in my ear while I softly moan in his. He carefully lowers me to the floor, facing up, then slams himself back inside me. No one has ever satisfied me the way he does. As that thought floats in my head, my center clenches around him, and I let out a loud moan. Jake takes a few more minutes then pulls out of me and leans against me, trying to catch his breath.

"Okay, I'm ready for my surprise now." I laugh.

"No time like the present, huh," he says, standing up and reaching for my hand.

I grab his hand, and he pulls me up. We get to the bedroom, and there is a box on the bed with a rose on top. Running over, I can hear Jake giggle because of how excited I still get when he brings me things. He says he does it so much because I am not the kind of woman who expects it, and it's always appreciated.

I tear open the box and see something red and tiny. I pull it out of the box only to be even more surprised when I see the matching red sparkling shoes underneath. "Baby, this is magnificent." I gawk, holding it to my body in front of the mirror.

"Try it on, my sweet girl," he says. He is standing behind me with the lust coming back to his eyes.

"I'll be right back." I turn to the bathroom with my dress and shoes in hand.

A minute later, I am dressed and feeling like the sexiest woman alive. The dress hugs every curve of my body, and the shoes are high, giving my butt a nice lift. Happy with the outcome, I open the door to Jake sitting on the edge of our bed, waiting in anticipation.

"Wow, baby. You look incredible," he states.

"Why did you get red?" I question. He knows I don't wear it much. It can be a dangerous color.

"Because it is a power color. Look at you. You are standing up straight. I can see the confidence bubbling in you." He stares at me with a devious smile as he stands behind me and rubs his hands gently up and down my arms. "I can't wait to rip this from your body later," he confesses, slowly showering my neck with the sweetness of his lips.

"Then let me take it off so I will have something nice to wear tonight." I push him back, giving his bulge a firm squeeze as I turn toward the bathroom to take it off.

Luca

"Sarah, please, calm down. You get so upset, and I didn't do anything wrong. What has been with you the last week?" I walk over to where she is crying on the bed.

"I can't. No, I won't do this anymore. I want a divorce. But you know that already, don't you? The papers were in the drawer of my nightstand, and now they aren't." She turns to face me, her eyes red and puffy with her nose matching. My heart breaks, knowing I never should have met with that woman I work with for drinks alone. Nothing happened but this is just the latest of my bad decisions.

"Nothing happened. I promise you," I try to explain for the millionth time. "I made a stupid decision. I never should have gone out for drinks with her without someone else there. I should have told you where I was going. I am so sorry."

"I want to trust you so badly, but this is not the first time I thought you cheated on me. Do you remember the waitress from the diner?" She pauses. "The way you looked at her and the look in her eyes when she saw you. Please just tell me the truth, Luca," she pleads.

"Sarah, I have never lied to you." I put my hand on her thigh, and she smacks it away.

"It's lying by omission," she bites back. "I love you, Luca. But I can't be with you if I can't trust you. I want you to sign the divorce papers and let me live my life."

"Can we just slow down?" I blurt out. Not that I am happy either, but there must be a way to fix this. I never cheated on her. I do love her. Isn't that all we need?

"Luca, you are never home." She sobs. When you are, you are either working out, eating, watching TV, or sleeping. We never do anything together. I just feel like you don't care about me unless you need me for sex. I just want to be happy, and I don't think I will be until we are through."

"I did see the papers while I was looking for the remote so I could watch TV. I knew you weren't happy, but I didn't know we had gotten to this point," I explain. "Please, don't do this. Not yet. Give me some time to fix this. I know I can be a better man and a better husband to you."

She turns on her back, and the tears fall from the outer corners of her eyes. Looking at me with a little bit of malice and a lot of hesitation, she tells me tonight is my last shot. "Ground rules for the reunion tonight: do not hug any of those women. I want you to introduce me to every woman you plan on saying hello to. And so help you God if you leave my side except to use the bathroom," she demands.

I smile and rub the inside of her upper thigh. "I like when you stand your ground. It turns me on," I tell her as my hand slides farther up her leg until I reach my destination. I lie on my side next to her and pull her closer while I try to help her stop crying. "I love you, Sarah," I whisper, kissing her pouty lips.

"I love you too." She moans as I take my fingers from her and lick them clean. I climb on top of her, parting her legs so I can taste her. I know she is still upset with me, but I also know she wants nothing more than to please me.

Her scent is sweet, and her taste is delicious. We haven't been together in some time, so I am going to take this slow. Not for me but for her. I feel awful for neglecting her for so long. Honestly, I didn't realize how long it had been. *Months. How did I let this happen?*

I make it up to her for a good half hour before she begs me to finish inside her, her legs shaking uncontrollably. I do as she asks, and then I scoop her off the bed and carry her into the shower with me. "I promise I will be a better man for you." I kiss her and proceed to soap up her loofa, and I take my time cleansing every inch of her.

Sunny

The rain is coming down hard when I talk Jake into leaving the reunion. Why they hold events like this at the end of March instead of when the weather is warmer, I will never understand. My head is pounding from the awful music, and my feet ache from my red sparkling high heels, which I never wear. It's late and the air is brisk as we run from the lounge to our car, which sits a few parking spots down. Jake unlocks my door and opens it as I hurry to get inside. He runs around the front of the car and hastily closes the door. His black suit is dripping, and my short red dress is clinging to my legs, so he starts the car so we can warm up.

I don't have the best memories from high school. I hear from so many that it was the best four years of their lives. I, on the other hand, hated all four years with equal disdain. I am a different type of person and always have been.

Most days, I was full of anxiety before I got out of bed in the morning because I didn't want to see Luca. He made me feel like crawling under a rock and dying. Now, with the help of my husband, I can control my anxiety, but I can still hear Luca in the back of my head, criticizing me. It makes me so unsure of myself, and sometimes it becomes crippling. I find myself staring out the window of our white coupe, quietly giving thanks those high school days are behind me.

I am still upset with myself that I let Jake talk me into going to this reunion. Most of our friends were there, and a lot of people who had moved away were there too. I was not expecting Luca to approach me tonight. As I watch him strut up to me, my body breaks into a panic. My palms become sweaty, and my body is cemented in place by fear. When Luca makes it to me, his presence paralyzes my body. Ugh, Luca. I could have gone a lifetime without seeing him again. His light blue eyes are deceiving and downright devious, but that suits him. He towers over me. Most people are taller than me, but he was big. He played sports, and it looks like he still works out every day. Usually, I can avoid him because Jake and I are close friends with Luca's friend Ryan. Thank God Jake recognizes him and rescues me before Luca can say anything.

Luca scares me, even though I'm fairly sure I was the only one to ever stand up to him. Tonight, when he first saw me, a smile covered his face, and his dimples stole the show. He is handsome, a creep, and a womanizer, but captivating all the same. From what I hear, not much has changed. He is married, although his wife looks like she's on another planet. I guess I can't blame her. I would too if my husband ran around with younger women. Ryan affirms the rumors are just that: rumors.

Jake puts his hand on my thigh, and the weight of his steady hand jolts me, my focus snaps back to reality. I turn and smile at him. He is my everything. I can't wait to get home so he can tear this dress off me. But after that, I have to tell him.

"You okay, sweet girl? You have been staring into space for a good ten minutes," he points out. The expression on his face is that of concern, though his smile is sweet as he looks at me before turning his eyes back to the road.

"I'm fine. It has been a long night." I yawn, putting my hand on top of his.

"Good. You seemed off ever since Luca came over and tried to talk to you."

"He's an ass."

"That's it, he an ass? He got a little close to you. Not to mention, your face lost all color when he made it to you," he argues, seeing the apparent lie all over my face. He knows I am far from exceptional. "Are you sure you are all right?"

"I am. I promise," I reassure him.

*****

We pull into the garden-lined asphalt driveway of our three-story Victorian. We had it renovated before we moved in three years ago. The outside is a muted dark blue with white shutters.

I never thought I would live in such an extravagant home. I love it, mainly because it is big enough for us to have a few kids.

Jake opens the large oak front door and steps aside so I can go ahead of him. I reach to the left of the door and turn the lights on. As we make our way upstairs to the master bedroom, he can tell I am not quite myself, so he does what he does best. He stops me as we enter the bedroom, lightly grabbing my arm. He turns me so we face each other. His eyes lock on to mine, and I get lost in him.

"Okay, my sweet girl. I am begging you. Tell me why you are so bothered by the fact that Luca tried to talk to you. Don't tell me you aren't. I know you better. You never told me exactly why you hate him so much," he says with a raised eyebrow.

His hands cup my face, holding me. Then his eyes are brimming with anger. He won't let this go because he sees I am upset. He hates when I'm angry. It's like he can feel the pain I feel and will do anything to make it stop.

I drop my arms to my sides, throw my head back, and bend my knees like a little kid that's getting frustrated. "He was my bully throughout high school. I saw him every day during those four miserable years. Every day for four miserable years, he was so mean. He always had something degrading to say to me. The reason why I struggle with my self-confidence, well, goes back to him. Not that my self-esteem was great, but he took what little of it I did have."

I feel the anxiety and anger rush through me. I can't move. I feel the sting of Luca's words lingering in my head. Great, I'm wide awake.

Jake takes his hands from my face and pulls me close. Burying my face in his neck, I take a deep breath. The smell of his cologne penetrates every inch of me. The heat coming from his body is melting my fears away, and I feel life return to my body. I feel so safe with him, his right hand holding the back of my head to his buff chest, his left pinning my body to his. Wrapping my arms around his waist, I let out a sigh, finding comfort in my favorite person.

He tucks my hair behind my shoulders, leans down, and whispers in my ear, "I love you more than life itself. I'm so sorry you had to deal with that bullshit. You are so beautiful. I love your long silky hair, your big brown eyes, and your sweet smile. I love your beautiful personality, and it doesn't hurt you have *the* finest ass in Rolling Hills."

I pull myself from him, and the hunger in his eyes catches me off guard, awakening the urge to let him do whatever he wants to me. I am taken over by desire as Jake manipulates his massive frame to compel me back toward our bed.

When we get to the edge of the bed, he is on top of me as we fall onto the soft white blanket that covers the sheets underneath. We are both smiling, and a giggle escapes my throat. His large body blankets mine with a comfortable weight that dissipates any remaining anxiety. I can feel his erection on the inside of my thigh as he rubs himself against me, never taking his lips from mine. I grab his brown hair and gently tighten my grip, groaning in anticipation. He stops and props himself up on his left elbow. He looks at me with a bashfulness I have never seen.

"What's wrong? Why did you stop? Why are you looking at me like that?" I question as I try to catch my breath.

"Do you remember about a month ago when we talked about starting a family?" he asks excitedly.

"Yes." I smile, recalling that night like it was five minutes ago. Having a baby with the only man, I believe, who will ever accept me for me. My body vibrates with excitement.

I lightly caress his stubble-dusted face. Then I take my index finger and follow the valleys of his body made by the mountains he calls muscles. My hand reaches the top of his pants, and I start to undo his belt. He started this, and my body doesn't want to wait.

"So I was thinking," he continues, keeping himself at bay until he can finish his thought. "Tonight would be a good night to start trying."

I can't believe what I am hearing. Butterflies have taken over my stomach, and now I know it's time to spill my secret. I can't stop the words. "Remember about a month ago when we talked about starting a family, and you picked me up, threw me over your shoulder, and carried me up here? Then you threw me on the bed and ravaged me?"

"Vaguely." He looks toward the ceiling like he's trying to remember, but the smile on his face gives him away.

"I was going to wait to make sure everything is okay before telling you, but we started a family that night." As soon as the words leave my lips, I freeze. My heart pounds in my chest, deafening my ears, and I can feel the hairs on the back of my neck stand up. I didn't think I would be this nervous about his reaction, but his silence is torture.

He just stares at me with his eyes bigger than I've ever seen. His mouth drops open, and with every passing second, I talk myself into the fact that he doesn't want kids at all. He is just saying that. I am experiencing the most uncomfortable silence I've ever had. I just want him to say something.

"Really?" Jake asks with an excited inflection in his voice.

I smile and nod, confirming that we are pregnant. Jake sits up and moves my tight red dress above my hips. He then gets back on top of me, pressing his soft lips against mine.

"I love you so much," he whispers as he pulls my panties down, tosses them on the floor, and slides his right hand up the inside of my thigh, taking his time reaching his destination. "You are so wet. I want you more than ever." He caresses around my entrance, teasing me until I am begging him for more.

"What do you need, my love? What do you want me to do to you?" he teases me as he lightly kisses my neck. All I can think is that he has already given me everything I wanted and some things I didn't know I wanted.

"Everything," I say breathlessly.

Jake knows what I like. Usually, Jake is rough—some would say dominating—but I love it. Tonight he is tender, his touch more possessive than usual.

Jake bites my bottom lip, causing me to wince in pain. Who am I trying to kid? I love it. Jake removes his fingers from me and spreads my legs with his knee so he can thrust himself inside of me. Jake feels like a cure for everything that ails me. My mind is blank, leaving me only able to feel him inside me. Between the heat radiating from him, the smell of his cologne, and the pure pleasure he brings, it feels like nothing can ever go wrong. Not with Jake's love. Our bodies become one with only sweat between us. I wrap my legs around his hips and pull him deeper while I pull his head down so I can devour his lips. We roll around the bed, taking in each other in every sense. He makes sure I am satisfied before he changes his pace so he can get his pleasure as well.

Jake falls over next to me, panting, with the biggest smile. My body is worn out and limp. I turn to him and can't help but laugh. He looks so satisfied.

"What?" he props himself up and looks at me, trying to catch his breath. His smile is unmistakable, and his eyes are barely open.

"I am so glad you are happy. I was afraid you didn't mean to start a family now."

"Are you kidding? I could not be more excited." He grabs my hand. "What can I do for you? Can I get you anything?" he asks, bringing my hand to his mouth and kissing my knuckles.

"I could go for some of that cookie dough ice cream in the freezer." My mouth waters at the thought.

"I ate the rest of that cookie dough when I stayed up late working the other night. I will go to Slims. I am almost positive they are still open. I can't let the mother of my child go to bed without ice cream," he insists.

Before I can veto the idea, Jake pushes himself off the bed and slides on a pair of jeans and a T-shirt. I look at him knowing how lucky I am, and my insides feel like I am finally whole. I wrap myself in a blanket and follow Jake down the grand staircase. At the bottom of the stairs, he turns to me and pulls me close to him. I am on the last step. Our foreheads touch as he steals one more kiss.

"What did I do to deserve you? I will be back with some cookie dough in a few minutes. I love you." He pulls his keys from his pocket and turns around, taking my hand as I follow behind him.

I walk him outside. "I love you too. Be careful, my love." But run back inside when the rain starts again.

I shut the door and head upstairs to take a shower. I can't wait for him to get back. I just want him to hold me for the rest of the night. At that thought, I smile like I just had sex for the first time. I get in the shower. I guess tonight didn't turn out so bad after all.

Luca

Sarah doesn't say a word the entire way home. Her blond hair hangs so I cannot see her face. It is how things are now and have been for a while. I focus on the road, trying to forget how numb I feel to her crazy accusations, and I am becoming numb to our deteriorating relationship. She is right; we need a divorce. This is toxic for me and Sarah. I tried to give us one more chance before I saw a divorce attorney.

I was never that great of a guy, but now she is being ridiculous. She knew what she was getting into when we got married. I love women, and I love to look at women. Nothing will change that. Besides, she rarely wants to have sex, and I am an addict. I just got lucky today. Our marriage has been in a downward spiral for a few years. I go through all the things I can change in my head, but I don't think she cares enough to try. This afternoon was for her, not because she wanted me or loves me. *Selfish bitch.*

It wasn't always like this. Sarah used to be happy with our life, but something in her changed in the last few years. She started becoming paranoid that I was having an affair, but I wasn't. I tried to reassure her. I tried over and over to prove my love for her to no avail. After I realized I couldn't make her as happy as she wanted to be, I started picking up more shifts at the fire station. I didn't necessarily want to be home with a woman who despises me. That's when things went from bad to worse.

I started drinking more and staying out late with the guys. She treats me as if I am doing something wrong, but I know she doesn't want me home. That much is clear. I have never cheated on her, even though the opportunity has presented itself more than a few times. I respect our vows more than that. Sarah says I'm full of shit. She swears I am having an affair. She has been upset since she saw me trying to apologize to a woman I wronged long ago.

Sarah and I never should have gotten married. We were young, and we both felt pressured by everyone, including our families. Don't get me wrong, I do have love for Sarah. She is paranoid, but I know she wants a reason to leave. I found divorce papers in the drawer of her night table last week. She has wanted to start a family for a long time, but I have been putting it off. Now she resents me for it. Do we want to bring children into our mess? I do not; that will not help anything. I have attempted to get her to see a therapist, but she refuses. She says I am heartless, even though I will be getting the divorce for her. I am not one to quit on things, no matter what they may be.

We pull up to our twenty-five-hundred-square-foot rancher, which was built by Sarah's grandfather and given to us as a wedding gift. I pull into the concrete driveway, parking in front of the two-car garage. My knuckles are white from my death grip on the steering wheel. I step out of my Jeep, and before I can open her door for her, she is halfway to the front door. She hurries to unlock it and runs inside, slamming the door in my face.

I open it, heavily irritated, and follow her to the eat-in kitchen. My body is tense, and I have had enough of this. I don't say anything because I have no idea what she is thinking. I pass her and go to the refrigerator to grab a soda. I stand up and turn toward her, just in time to duck an incoming assault.

"What the fuck? Flirting with some little bitch. How long have you been fucking that one?" Sarah shrieks as she hurls the water bottle at my head.

"I was not flirting with her. I—" I duck, the water bottle missing me by a half inch. It hits the door of the refrigerator with a loud smack. I am surprised it didn't break. Rage starts to knot in my stomach. *This bitch.* I swallow my anger and remember I cannot lose it on her. I control my fury enough to stay silent. I am going to tell her she can have her divorce as soon as she finishes her rant. I am done.

"Why do you hate me?" Her lips tremble, and her eyes flood with tears.

"Sarah, it's not what you think. Please listen to me." I walk toward her slowly with my hands up, letting her know I am not that angry with her. Her rage and jealousy are unwavering. "We need to talk this through. I can explain," I plead with her, squashing my urge to laugh at the thought of me flirting with Sunny Thompson. Is it that crazy though? Yes, it is.

"Fuck you, Luca. I can't take this anymore. You would rather flirt with some girl at a high school reunion when you promised you wouldn't leave my side." Her voice cracks in anger. "I know about your little eighteen-year-old on the side too. I am done fighting for your attention. I'm leaving!"

Her face is red with fury. She breaks my gaze, turns around, and grabs her keys, which are sitting on the living room table. Before I can get to her, she is running out of the front door, slamming it. And then I hear her car screech out of the driveway.

*****

After Sarah storms out, I pour myself a scotch. I should have had an affair; it is ruining my marriage anyway. I know she is talking about the young woman who showed up at the firehouse with cookies a few weeks ago. There had been a fire two months ago in the woman's apartment building.

Ryan, Jimmy, four others, and I happened to be working that day. A call came in around two in the afternoon that one of the buildings at Swan Circle Apartments was on fire, and it was spreading fast. When we got to the apartment complex, the building was engulfed in flames, and smoke was billowing out from every direction. The three of us finished gearing up so we could start a search for anyone still inside. I felt a light tug on my arm. I turned and saw an older woman with her lips pinched and her eyes squinting as if she didn't want me to see the terror in her eyes. She informed me there was a young woman that lived on the third floor. Her car was in the parking lot, but she was nowhere to be seen. I gave everyone the heads-up to keep an eye out.

Once inside, the heat and smoke became worse, even though the vent team did their best to ventilate the building before we got in. We started on the second floor, where the fire started. Some brainiac threw water on a grease fire. The smoke was dark and thick, and the fire was spreading rapidly. We did not have much time to find her or anyone else who might still be in here. Once we swept the second floor and all was clear, we headed up to where the young girl might be.

As we headed up the stairs, the smoke got thicker. We kept a close eye on the ever-changing situation. The fire itself had not made it past the second floor, but that could change in an instant. They did renovations not long ago. Hopefully, the contractor was careful and sealed everything so the fire could not spread inside the walls. Things could go from bad to worse fast.

When we reached the third floor, we headed straight to the last apartment on the left, where the terrified old woman said the girl lived. The heat grew with every passing second. Ryan pulled his sleeve up and put his arm against the door to see if it was hot. We tried the knob, but it was locked. Ryan took the Halligan and placed it in the doorjamb so I could hit it with the flathead ax. The door opened. We had been in for eight minutes, and we needed to find her. We needed to be quick.

I went in and headed to the right where the living room was, but I didn't see anyone. I let Ryan and the guys know what I was seeing. So far, nothing. Ryan's flashlight was illuminating the room through the smoke, making it a little easier to see. I heard "all clear" coming over the radio again when I heard our commander tell us we needed to move and we didn't have much time left. I turned the corner and went into the bedroom, where I saw an arm sticking out from under the bed. I pulled her out and scooped her up like a baby, letting her know I got her. Suddenly, I heard her door slam, and Jimmy said we couldn't go out that way. Her living room was in flames. We had to go through the window. Between the fire alarm blaring, the smoke, and all the commotion, this girl was petrified.

We all huddled on the floor under her bedspread as they broke the glass so we could get the hell out of there. We got her out first. I will never forget the look on her face. I don't think I have ever seen anyone that scared in my life.

Back at the station, I had a headache, and my stomach was in knots thinking about the girl we rescued. Before I left, I found my captain and asked if there was any word on the young woman. He lowered his head, and his voice was rough. "Not yet. I will keep you posted. Go home and get some rest, Monts. You boys did well today." He patted my shoulder, and I decided to follow his orders.

I called Sarah to pick me up, and she cried as I told her about the insane day I had. I didn't go into too much detail because, though she doesn't love me, she doesn't want me dead either. Later that day, I got a call from my captain informing me that the young woman we rescued had survived and would make a full recovery. I am sure it was the exhaustion, but I recall tears falling from my eyes at the news.

A few weeks later, a beautiful woman with a tiny frame and a big chest strutted into the firehouse with dozens of homemade cookies. The small woman introduced herself as Maisy, and she had, beyond a doubt, made a full recovery. I had no idea how lovely she was. All I saw that day was a scared little girl in my arms. Her red hair was long, and her green eyes were bright.

Maisy explained that when she was anxious—which was all the time now—she baked. She was grateful for the three of us saving her life, and she thought we should reap the benefits. It was the best I had felt in a long time: appreciated.

Sarah happened to walk in at the exact moment Maisy gave me a thank-you hug after Ryan and Jimmy got theirs. Of course, Sarah's jealousy emanated from her entire being. I introduced them, explaining why Maisy was here, but Sarah was convinced I was sleeping with her.

Rubbing the memory from my eyes, I saunter into the living room and drop heavily on the oversized beige couch that Sarah "couldn't live without." I kick off my dress shoes and lean back, resting my head on the edge of the cushions. I rub my forehead, trying to dull the headache I can feel creeping up while swirling the scotch before I enjoy it. I then head to bed.

I think about how Sarah never trusted me, even when we first got together. I looked but I never touched anyone. I can't believe she thought I was flirting with Sunny earlier tonight. That blows my mind. Even if I were to have an affair, it sure as hell would not be with Sunny.

I never told Sarah how I treated Sunny, how I hurt her. I wanted to apologize to Sunny tonight, but her husband, Jake, came over before I had the chance. He looked protective of her when he saw me from the bar, where he was ordering two drinks. I guess he didn't like how close I stood to her because he weaved his way to us within seconds. I felt a strange connection to her, like a magnetic pull. She smelled of lavender, and her energy was as radiant as ever.

She looked as though she saw a ghost when I walked up to her. Our eyes met, and it was like neither of us could look away. Sunny looked intimidated, and I could feel myself start to get aroused. What the hell? It's Sunny. I am not into her. She did look amazing in that little red number she had on. If she dressed like that in high school, maybe things would have been different between us.

Sipping my scotch, my thoughts drift from Sunny to my wife.

Thinking about how things started with Sarah, I know I need to sign the divorce papers. It is time. I want her to be happy. I will sign them and leave them on the kitchen table for her. I'll pack some things tonight and stay at a hotel for a while.

About twenty minutes later, my cell rings, and I jump at the sudden noise that fills the room. I don't recognize the number, but I hope it is Sarah so I can tell her my decision and she can come home. I put my scotch on the table in front of me and pick up the phone.

Sunny

The warm water holds me steady and washes away the feelings I had earlier, but it leaves the warmth of Jake all over me. I wash my hair with my favorite lavender shampoo and revel in the fact that Jake is as excited as I am to start a family. I can't stop thinking about how lucky I am. I have never been this happy. Rinsing the shampoo out and applying the conditioner, I let my past go down the drain.

I wasn't the happiest person up until I met Jake. I struggled with depression and crippling anxiety since I was young. I guess it wasn't until I turned twenty-one that I had taken my mental health more seriously. I realized that it would never go away, and I was tired of feeling like crap and being too anxious to be able to leave my house.

I finish up and turn the water off. I grab a towel from the hook on the wall and wrap myself up. It has been a good twenty minutes since Jake left, and Slims was just around the corner. I start to get worried, but I remember to breathe. I know I worry over nothing most of the time. Maybe Slims is busy with other ice cream cravings. I walk into the bedroom when I hear my phone ring.

*****

I throw on yoga pants and a T-shirt then slide into my sneakers. I almost fall down the stairs, unable to control what my body is doing. I grab my keys from the dish on the hallway table and run to my little sports car. I try to start my car, not realizing how much my body is shaking until I try to put the key in the ignition.

The drive to the hospital seems like it is another state away, but in reality, only takes about five minutes.

I see the signs for parking by the ER. I turn off the car and grab my purse from the seat next to me. I can feel the undigested food from dinner rising in my throat as my muscles tense. My vision is blurry from the never-ending river of tears. I stop at the guard station and open my mouth to speak, but nothing comes out. I must look like death because the guard stands up and puts his hand on my shoulder as if to steady me.

"Miss, are you okay? Are you hurt?" the young man asks. He is tall and looks genuinely worried. I look at his name tag pinned to his blue uniform to try to give myself something to focus on so I can get my thoughts straight. Frazier—his last name is Frazier.

"I-I-My husband. I got a call." This is all I can force out.

"Okay. Go through those double doors and stop at the nurses' station straight down the hall. They will be able to give you more information."

He lets go of my shoulder and gives me a sympathetic smile. I turn and go through the double doors, heading to the nurses' station. I stop and a young woman with her dark hair in a bun looks up. I tell her why I am here, and she instructs me to go across the hall to the waiting room. She says she will let Dr. Malone know I am here.

I take a seat in an uncomfortable gray chair. My mind is going in a million directions, not being able to focus on anything. It feels as though time stopped.

Dr. Malone finally comes out about fifteen minutes later. He takes a seat in the chair facing mine. My heart drops as I wait to find out what is going on. I look at the doctor, an older man. His hair is white, and his voice is strong and steady.

"Mrs. Thompson," he starts, "your husband has been in a car accident that has left him with some serious injuries. He has a ruptured spleen, a lacerated liver, and a punctured lung. He also has some swelling around his brain. We are doing everything we can."

I stare at him blankly, not being able to believe what the doctor told me. I think about all the injuries Dr. Malone said Jake had. The only picture in my head is of Jake bloody and broken because someone lost control of their car. A woman, Dr. Malone told me, is also in surgery with severe injuries.

"Mrs. Thompson, do you understand what I just told you?"

I look through him like he isn't there and nod my head. He puts his hand on my knee and says he will let me know more as soon as he can. He stands up and leaves the waiting room.

I hear a commotion at the nurses' station, but I don't care enough to see what is going on. Then he walks in with overpowering energy. Are you kidding? What the hell is he doing here?

Then it hits me. His wife must be the woman in surgery who hit Jake.

Luca

"Hello?"

"This is Dr. Rossinger of the Rolling Hills General Hospital. Luca Claymont please."

"This is Luca. Is everything okay, Doctor?"

"I'm sorry to inform you, your wife, Sarah, has been in a car accident. She is in surgery now. We need you to come to the hospital right away."

"What happened? Is she okay?" My heart starts to race, my body tenses, and beads of sweat form on my forehead.

"From what the police have told us, she lost control of her car and struck another car. It is important for you to get to the hospital right away, Mr. Claymont."

"Okay, I am on my way now."

I drop the phone, and I grab my keys off the table. The hospital is only a few minutes away. I know this is my fault. If only I were a better husband. Had we gotten a divorce when things started to go south… I knew my selfishness would cause her pain, but not like this. *Fuck. Fuck. Fuck.*

My entire body trembles with anger toward myself for letting her leave when she was so upset. I pull into the ER entrance parking lot and jump out of my car, slamming the door. My strides are quick with purpose. I run inside past the security guard, and I plow through the double doors to the nurses' station. I hear the guard yelling something, but my pounding heart drowns every other noise out. There are a few young nurses gathered around.

A young nurse with blond hair turns to me and flashes a bright smile and asks how she can help me.

I am out of breath and barely able to ask her where my wife is. She tells me to take some deep breaths so I can catch my breath and tell her what I need. Her bossy attitude annoys me, but she has a point. I can't breathe. After I calm down, I organize my thoughts enough to explain I had gotten a call that Sarah had been in a car accident and is in surgery.

"Are you Mr. Claymont?" the nurse asks.

I shake my head yes.

"Sarah is still in surgery. Please have a seat in the waiting room across the hall. I'll let Dr. Rossinger know you are here."

"Thank you. As soon as you know something, please—"

"I will have the doctor speak with you as soon as he can. Please have a seat." She kindly points to the drab tiny room across the hall.

My heart drops as I walk into the small waiting room. Then I see her: Sunny Thompson.

I have a sick feeling in my gut that Jake is the one Sarah hit. Sunny is wearing black yoga pants and an oversized sweatshirt. Her knees are pulled up to her chest, where her head is resting. She looks up at me through the mess of brown hair covering her face and bloodshot eyes.

"Luca? What are you doing here?" Her voice cracks. She looks distracted and out of it.

"I got a call that Sarah was in a car accident," I explain. "All I know is that she is in surgery. Nothing else. She stormed out of the house after we got into a huge fight."

Sunny gives me a crooked look.

"This is all my fault," I say, turning and slamming my fist into the vending machine that sits against the wall.

Sunny starts to sob again.

I take a seat in the uncomfortable gray chair next to her. "What are you doing here?" I need to know if Sarah hit Jake.

"I got a phone call that Jake was in a car accident and is in surgery. Same as you. The doctor came out a little while ago. Jake has a ruptured spleen and a list of other issues that I forgot after they told me they weren't sure if he would make it." Sunny starts to choke on her tears, and she puts her head down.

I can see her body shaking. I put my arm around her and try to comfort her, but she pushes me away. I feel responsible for making her cry yet again. Back in school, I got off seeing her upset, but not for the reason she thinks. At this moment, I want to be there for her, and she wants no part of it.

We sit in uncomfortable silence for over an hour until one doctor appears in the doorway. He does not look relieved or ready to tell either of us good news. I squeeze Sunny's shoulder and whisper that the doctor has come in. She looks at me with dead eyes, as if she knew what they were going to say. She was always weird like that. Dr. Malone walks over to where we are sitting and sits in front of us.

"Jake didn't make it, did he?" Sunny choked out before Dr. Malone could say a word.

"His injuries were extensive. We did everything we could. I'm so sorry, Mrs. Thompson. Give us a few minutes, and one of the nurses will bring you back to see him."

Sunny sits back down next to me and waits. Still no word on Sarah.

"And Sarah?" I ask.

"I'm sorry, Mr. Claymont. She is still in surgery as far as I know. Dr. Rossinger will be out as soon as he can."

Just then, Dr. Rossinger appears from the hall, and I stand up to meet him, but I knew I would get the same news as Sunny.

"Mr. Claymont, I am so sorry to tell you Sarah didn't make it. I will have someone bring you back to her shortly."

*****

The room is gray and cold. It looks like a bomb exploded. The brightness of the fluorescents makes me squint as they burn my eyes. Sarah is lying on a table in the middle, surrounded by a mess of monitors that are now off, under a white sheet covering everything but her face. The light above her makes her look like a sleeping angel.

I sit on a stool by her bed and pick up her hand, wanting nothing more than for her to wake up. I can't fix this. I know this is karma for not doing the right thing—ever. Probably for all the messed-up stuff I have done in my life. I hold her limp hand in mine, and the sharpest pain I have ever felt bolts through my heart like lightning. I will never forgive myself for destroying her.

I remember the day I saw Sarah for the first time. She was playing tennis at the racquetball club I used to frequent. Her long blond hair was up in a perfect ponytail. Her never-ending legs were barely covered by her short white skirt. She looked at me with the greenest eyes I had ever seen and a smile that I couldn't resist. I recall feeling the need to have her almost instantly. Her father was my racquetball partner for a year before I asked to meet her.

"Sarah, I am so sorry I upset you. It's my fault this happened. All you had to do was come home. I would have given you the divorce. You could have started over."

Tears fall from my eyes, and my heart shatters. I feel as though I am suffocating, fighting for every breath. I never knew I had the emotions I now feel sitting beside my wife, knowing she would not be coming back to me. I am out of time; there is no making things right with her.

I sit here for about a half hour and then move a few strands of hair from her forehead, bending over to give the one I truly let down a final kiss.

Sunny

My stomach is knotted with anxiety and fear as I walk into the room where Jake is. I am in shock. Even seeing him on the operating table, I still can't wrap my head around what happened. He looks as though he will turn and look at me. I am waiting for him to laugh and say "got ya." It doesn't happen. All because of some fucking cookie dough ice cream. All because he wanted to make me happy. That was all he ever wanted.

He bought me an old two-story building in the town square to turn it into an art gallery and studio. We named it The Muse because he told me I was his muse. He said I inspired him to live a fuller life, and we were trying to make it more so.

I looked forward to our morning ritual. He got up a half hour before I did. As I opened my heavy eyelids, I would see him in front of the tall mirror at the foot of the bed. He would have his back to me so that I could see everything. His big brown eyes were always fixed on me. His hair slicked back, honey-colored skin kissed by the sun coming through the window. When he pulled his slacks up, he would gaze at me through his reflection on the mirror, and a dirty smile would take over his face. Then he would come over to where I lay and kiss me. He would then turn, grab his dress shirt, and head to our lavish bathroom. He was a master of foreplay. He knew I would not be able to concentrate on my work because I would be fantasizing about him. Some mornings, he would let me twist his arm to come back to bed before he left.

I now take his hand in mine and rub the inside of his palm. I used to do this when he couldn't relax. Now I'm sitting here, wondering how I'm going to get through my days without him. How am I supposed to raise a child on my own?

I have help at the gallery. I hired a woman named Ann, who also rents the second floor of the gallery. Jake and I renovated the gallery space right after we finished the house. After the renovations were finished, I had a show that featured local artists, and the proceeds went to a marketing fund for them. That was a happier time in life, and now it was all changing over ice cream.

I feel my throat closing, and tears flood my eyes. I put my head down, not being able to let go of him. My body trembles as I sit here, unable to say goodbye, and I think about being in that big house all by myself. I don't want to go back there tonight, but it is late, and I have nowhere to go. Mel, my best friend, is on a business trip, and I can't think of anyone I want to be around. I could go to my studio in the gallery. I have a twin mattress there for when I work late and am too tired to drive home, but that's it. Maybe I'll stay in the motel on the main road. Everything will remind me of him no matter where I go. I can't run from what happened tonight.

Not to mention, of all people to be here now, is Luca. I know I can't ask him to be there for me; he just lost his wife. He's a piece of shit anyway. And as bad as I feel, I can't imagine him to be any bit sane.

I can't fathom what his wife must have gone through. Having a man who is as arrogant as he is good-looking is tough on a woman's heart. Even in high school, he was a dog, and he treated women like shit. *No. No. No. This will be easier if I process this alone.*

I take a deep breath, grabbing Jake's still warm hand. Putting his fingers to my trembling lips, I tell Jake how much I love him, how much better he made my life. I stand up and walk out of the room, feeling as though I left most of myself in the chair next to Jake, yet weighed down by a force I cannot see. As I make my way down the hall, I brush my fingertips along the wall beside me. I can't think or feel. Numbness fills me until I feel nothing except the warmth of my tears staining my cheeks.

I look to my right and see Luca kiss his wife on her forehead. For the first time, I feel terrible for him. I never knew he had emotions. He was always so cold—to me at least. I want to stop staring, but I can't.

He turns and sees me. He makes his way to me and throws his arm around my shoulder as we leave and try to live past tonight.

Luca

I stand up to leave. When I turn toward the door, I see Sunny at the window to Sarah's room. I walk out, and without a word, I put my arm around her as we walk toward the exit doors of the ER. When we get to the parking lot, we stop. She breaks free of my hold on her and turns toward me. She wipes the tears from her face and stares at me for a minute, making me feel a little vulnerable. I was used to doing that to people, not the other way around. Her arms are crossed, and I am getting ready for her to flip out. My arms are in my pockets as I try to look as relaxed as possible, but I can feel pain in my jaw from clenching my teeth.

"I am sorry about Sarah," she says. "You going to be okay?"

"Yeah, I'll be fine," I lie. "I'm sorry about Jake. Do you need a ride home?"

I know she will say no, but I offer regardless. I owe it to Sunny anyway, and I owe her a lot more than just a ride home. It is not the time to ask for her forgiveness. That will have to wait. Maybe I won't bother asking at all. I tried to apologize to her less than twelve hours ago, and now both of us have suffered. Everyone has suffered.

"No, thank you. I drove here so…thanks though." She turns and starts sulking away.

I can't leave it like this; it feels wrong. Just because I lost Sarah does not mean I can't be the man I know I should be. Without another thought, I take a few steps to catch up to her, and I grab her upper arm, pulling her close to me. I can smell the lavender coming off her. "Give me your phone," I say to her as I pull mine out of my pocket and hold it out for her to take.

"Why?" she demands, pulling away from my grip on her arm.

"In case you need anything, or in case I need anything," I try to explain.

After a few minutes of debating whether or not to oblige, she sighs in defeat.

"Here," she grunts, handing her phone over and snatching mine. "I really can't see what I would need from you." Her voice is weak. "My husband is gone, and you want to be something more than the asshole you are?" Her tone changes, piercing every fiber of my being. "Your wife just died. Maybe you could act upset instead of trying to take me home. You are a fucking creep," she screams, pushing me hard for the tiny thing she is.

I know she is angry and upset, so I let her yell. I also know I deserve it. When she finishes yelling, she grabs her phone out of my hand and throws mine into my chest. I catch it against my sweatshirt, not understanding how she thinks I am being a creep at the moment. She takes a deep breath and closes her eyes as if trying to ground herself.

"I'm sorry, Luca. I shouldn't have yelled or questioned how you feel right now. I'm so sorry." At that, she turns and walks away.

Dumbfounded by this confusing interaction, I get in my Jeep and pull the door shut. The seat hugs my exhausted body. As I take a deep breath, all I can smell is Sarah's perfume from earlier that night. I bought her this particular perfume two Christmases ago. It smells like strawberries.

I look at the clock on the dash and can't believe it is 4:00 a.m. already. I sit for a while, my head resting on the back of the seat, trying to make some sense of everything that happened. I realize nothing will make sense, so I start driving. I have no destination, but I am not ready to go home to a place that will never be the same.

Luca

I decide to check on Sunny after I hadn't heard from her since every-thing that happened two weeks ago. I did see her at Sarah's funeral, but she stayed in the back, and I didn't get a chance to thank her for being there. Just as well, I think. I was in no shape to talk to anyone. The next day, I ended up going to Jake's as well. I understand now why Sunny kept to herself at Sarah's. It was overwhelming. Just the guilt I carry is overwhelming—to know this was my fault, even if indirectly.

I waited two weeks so we would both have time to mourn and get ourselves to the point of being able to leave the house. My best friend, Ryan, who is a friend of Sunny's as well, has been checking on her and keeping me informed on how she is doing. I know it sounds borderline stalking, but I feel responsible for so much of her sadness. It is my responsibility to make sure she is safe even if she hates me. Hopefully, that will change. Ryan swears I am doing this because I am finally coming to terms with the fact that I have a thing for her.

I get off work early, so I go to the local coffeehouse, Always Brewin', and grab two vanilla crème lattes. Then I head over to The Muse. Spring is finally in full swing, so I decide to walk since it's only a few blocks. The sun is warm on my face, and it feels good to get some fresh air. We have been slow at work, which is good, but I need to get outside. I honestly need the walk to figure out what I am going to say to Sunny when I get there. I don't know why I am having such a hard time with this. I am usually the calm one, the confident one. Today, however, I feel like the nerds I used to torture in school: scared.

I get to the gallery and stand outside, looking at the front of the building. It is white with some large black letters spelling The Muse. There are small rounded black awnings that cover each of the five windows—two long windows on the first floor and three regular-sized windows on the second. It is very high-end and appeals to the like.

When I pull the door open, I hear a little bell chime. I step inside, but I don't see anyone. The coffee is warm in my hands, making them sweat. I haven't been inside this building since her husband bought it. The inside looks amazing, wholly renovated. The hardwood floors look bold against the stark white walls. A counter serves as a catch-all on the right and temporary walls up making a sort of maze. There are paintings from Sunny's previous art show still up. From what Ryan told me, she hasn't been here much, but she told him she would be here today. She is planning a show that will open in a few months.

I look around, weaving through the temporary walls, and stumble upon some of her pieces. They are stunning. She always had talent. I could tell which ones belonged to preaccident Sunny and then postaccident Sunny. Her postaccident paintings are sad, angry, and very dark. I didn't know she had this side to her.

I hear a door open, throwing me back into my dilemma of what to say. I turn around, and she appears from a back room. My eyes settle on her captivating smile. Her smile could light up the world. Her eyes could see inside your soul like she knew everything without you telling her. I step toward her. Her smile fades, and her eyes lose their sparkle. At this moment, it hits me how much I affected her, and not in a positive way. I hand her the vanilla latte in hopes we can be civil.

"I figured maybe we could talk," I start.

Sunny takes the coffee, but she won't look at me.

"Yeah? What do you want to talk about?" Her voice is soft and timid. She still will not meet my eyes, but she takes the coffee. After a few seconds, she finally looks up and studies my face, still feeling the need to guard herself.

"Are you okay?" I ask, trying to break the ice, trying to get her to understand that I am sorry. I do care what happens to her, and I want to try to make things up to her. If I can get her to open up a little, I will have my chance at redemption. I still have no idea why

I feel the need for her forgiveness. While I was home the week after the accident, I decided to be a better man. I couldn't do it in time for Sarah, but I will not make the same mistake twice.

She takes a deep breath. "I'm okay. You?" Her throat tightens, and she is barely able to get the words out. She rubs the lid of the cup between her thumb and forefinger.

"I've been okay." I smile, trying not to upset her. "I wanted to apologize for everything."

Sunny rolls her eyes and looks down at the floor.

"Apologize? For what?" Her eyes start to fill with tears. Her eyes focus back on me with what I can only describe as deadly contempt. She continues, "How you used to make me feel like I was worth nothing when we were in school? Do you have any idea what you did to me? Taking every shred of self-confidence I had? My life, after you started your shit, got worse. I thought I was worthless, and not to mention the things I did because of it. I did everything I could do to prove to myself that I was desirable instead of how you made me feel. It took a long time to forget your voice in my head. I still hear you criticizing me whatever I'm doing—picking out something to wear or deciding on what to paint. I ask myself how you would react to it. Do you have any idea what that is like?

"Or would you like to apologize because your wife took away the one person who made me feel safe and who accepted everything about me, no matter what? What, exactly, would you like to apologize for?" Sunny hissed, visibly a mess and not handling things at all.

I could feel my blood pressure rising, and anger hit me like a tsunami. I want to choke her. Who the fuck does she think she is? I know I said some hurtful things to her, apparently more harmful, but she needs to let that go. It was a long time ago. *Breathe. Just walk away. Don't lose it.*

"You know what, Sun? Forget I came by. You do know I fucking lost my wife too. Things haven't been easy for me either. I thought maybe we could help each other, but it's clear you don't feel the same. See you around." I turn, drop my coffee in the trash, and walk out.

*****

Scrolling through my phone, I study the sympathy messages from the barely legal that quietly passed their phone numbers to me while no one was looking. I can't say I mind the attention. After Sarah's funeral, I didn't know what to do with myself, so I embraced my inner womanizer. The sympathy squad has been offering a warm, moist place to hide, and I've been taking full advantage.

The one with the red hair, Ms. Maisy, ends all of her texts with two red hearts. She is my favorite at the moment. I have taken her out a few times. She is shy, so she is nervous about doing some things for me, but we will get there.

The blonde, Ms. Golden Showers, is crazy in all the wrong ways. She messages me every day and is starting to get on my last nerve. I have told her I don't want anything serious, but she is young and thinks I will change my mind. Golden Showers is adventurous. She likes to please me, but I may have to cut her loose shortly.

Legs is a good time. Although she is a couple of years older than the others, she can't seem to keep my cock out of her mouth. I've never finished while getting my dick sucked, but she works some magic. She chokes just about every time, but that's because I give her no warning, and I push her head closer to me then explode down her throat. Legs is starting to understand the pattern; she's getting better at knowing when it's going to happen.

The sweet one reminds me of Sunny in high school. She has the same carefree attitude as Sunny. I am drawn to Sweetie more than the others. She and I cuddle, and she always has a solution to fix my mood. She likes it when I take control of her and do whatever comes to mind, yet there are still some things these girls won't try.

Tonight I am taking a new sympathy message to dinner. Sympathy's message said she got my number from Maisy. We will go to dinner in the city, and then we will see what this one will do. The only things I have gathered are that she is twenty and has an attitude. *What is her name? Amy? Annie? Whatever. She will end up with a nickname by the end of tonight.*

Tossing my phone onto the bed, I strip my clothes off and head toward the bathroom Sarah always dreamed of having. I turn the shower on and step into the scalding water, hoping it will relax my aching body and the headache from hell. I close my eyes, and Sunny creeps into my mind. The way she looked at me when I walked into The Muse, her shattered heart displayed for me to see—it is all etched into my brain. Sunny tries to hide how she feels but fails miserably. I can still see the storm brewing in her eyes as I apologized to her, a mix of hate, hurt, worry, and anger. I wash my face, hoping it will erase Sunny's gloomy look.

When all else fails, take a dumb girl out and screw her until you feel better. Stepping out of the shower, I know this cocky bitch will get more than she can handle, and I'm excited about it. There is nothing better than using a girl who is a crappy person. I won't feel bad when I stop talking to her.

Luca

I roll up to Ms. Attitude's house, and there she is. Her little black number rides up her legs as she hurries down the stone walkway. She yanks the passenger door open and climbs in next to me, shooting me a look I can only describe as sassy. *Sassy*—that name suits her. As soon as she opens her mouth, I dislike her. She babbles about things I couldn't care less about, touching my arm every time the opportunity presents itself. Her voice is shrill, and her sassiness is not helping her cause. That's okay; she won't be talking all night. *I've got something that will shut her up.*

I pull into a parking space close to the entrance of my favorite Mexican restaurant.

Hopping out and rounding the back of the car, I am thankful for a moment where I can't hear her yapping. I pull the passenger door open so that Sassy can jump out. I hold my hand out for her, and she grabs it without hesitation, refusing to let go. I shut the door with my other hand, and we head inside.

The lighting is soft, casting the perfect light on the hostess's ass as she guides us to our table. Sassy catches me, and the way her mouth curls and her eyes glare at me makes it clear I will get what I want tonight. I miss the feeling of girls doing whatever it takes to get what they want. That dirty thought causes me to relax and squeeze Sassy's hand, making sure she knows she has nothing to worry about. At least for tonight.

For the next hour, I pretend to be interested in all the things she is saying, but at least she is doing most of the talking. Minimal effort on my part is just the right amount. She goes on about her family, college, and her job that "pays for her shoes" that she hates. None of this is holding my interest. All I can think about is her mouth around my cock.

I motion to the waiter for our check. I'm tired of tonight's charade. "You ready to get out of here?" I propose. A simple "sure" slips between her lips.

On the way back to my house, Sassy is quiet for the first time all night. It makes me wonder if she is up for this. Only one way to find out, I guess. I open the car door for her, and we head to the front door. Her body visibly stiffens as I push the front door open. I ask if I can take her coat, and she slides out of the only piece of clothing genuinely covering any part of her.

I ask if she wants something to drink as I stalk closer to her, enjoying the fact that she looks terrified. Sassy shakes her head no. Reaching her, I grab a handful of her hair and pull her head back as I lean down and swallow her lips. She lets out a breathy sigh when I pull away and start working my way down her neck. I reach for her large nipples and bite them harder than I usually would. I don't like her, and seeing her uncomfortable is making this encounter even more enjoyable.

I straighten her back up and then guide her on to her knees while I unzip my pants and pull my dick out for her. When she slides her lips around my cock, she chokes at first then relaxes her throat for my size. Once she gets used to me, I start to pound my cock in and out of her mouth while her hair is tight in my hand so she can't pull away. Before I cum in her mouth, I pull out and flip her against the floor. I push her legs open.

"You okay?" I check to make sure before I break her.

She looks at me, nods, and says, "Yeah."

I dive back into her neck while wrestling with the condom wrapper. Then, without warning, I slam my girth inside of her, pushing out a scream muffled by my hand. Her eyes open wide, and her body tightens beneath me. I ask her if she is okay, not taking my hand from her mouth. Again, she nods.

"Do you like it when it hurts?"

Another nod.

As I ask her more questions to see how far I can push her, the slicker her center becomes. Whispering terrible things in her ear, I can't help but want to rip her apart. I pound into her hard and fast, not heeding her body's need for me to let up. I tell her I want to cum all over her, and her eyes relax, looking as though she is relieved I am just about done with her.

I remove my hand from her mouth, and her chest rises and falls as she tries to catch her breath. I pull out of her, immediately realizing that the condom broke. *Fuck!*

Sliding off her, I get to my feet. Feeling no remorse and satisfied, I look down at her and blurt out, "The condom broke. Go clean yourself out."

"Are you kidding me?" she shrieks. Her eyes fill with tears, and it finally dawns on her what tonight was all about. She jumps up with her lips pinched and her brows drawn together in heated disdain, and she snatches her clothes off the floor. She takes off to the bathroom in such a huff that she almost trips on the lace panties around her ankle.

Wonder if she's feeling sassy now?

I can hear the water in the bathroom turn on, and she peeks her head out and asks meekly if I have some soap she can use. I push myself from my bed and grab a lavender bar of soap from the linen closet. I drop my shoulders and cautiously walk toward her and give her the soap.

"Not expecting all that, huh?" I try to lighten the mood and realize I'm not helping. "Are you okay?"

She reassures me she is okay, shutting the door in my face. The water turns back on, and I retreat to my bed.

She emerges fifteen minutes later looking like a shell of what she did earlier. She smiles as I pick her up and lay her gently down and climb in beside her. Sassy scoots over to me and tries to get as close as possible. I wrap my arm around her, pulling her in while I stroke her hair. I feel her looking up at me, and I know this means she wants some after-sex affection from me, but that is not what this is supposed to be. Being me, I play her game and give her a soft forehead kiss.

At that moment, my phone is buzzing beside me. I relieve Sassy of my hold and look at the message. She is not going to be happy, but I need to go to sleep. "I called you a cab. It is waiting outside to take you home."

"What the hell is wrong with you?" she bellows, jumping up from the bed. "What kind of jerk are you? You just had your way with me, and you call me a damn *cab*." Sassy's eyes are narrow, her mouth gaping open as if I killed her dog. "Fuck you, Luca."

She storms out of my room, and I hear her as she stomps toward the front door. I fly out of bed when I hear glass breaking, not once but twice. *What the hell is this whore doing?*

I reach the living room just as she slams the door shut, and I see Sarah's favorite vases shattered into millions of pieces. I have half a mind to follow the sassy whore home. My anger toward Sassy is indescribable as I cannot help but punch a hole through the wall, picturing Sassy's face.

My anger is getting me nowhere, and this is what I was trying to avoid. I told Sassy I wasn't looking for anything serious. I grab the broom and dustpan from the hall closet and clean up the broken pieces of Sarah. Things in my life seem to shatter quite often.

Sunny

About two months after the accident, I start feeling somewhat like myself. I don't spend as much time in bed. Instead, I go to the gallery as much as possible. Unfortunately, this week, I have been under the spell of incredible sadness. I ended up staying in the safety of my bed for most of it. Even today, my eyelids are as weighted as sandbags, and my bones feel like lead.

Not long ago, I started going to a support group for young adults who have lost their spouses. I realized, after Luca left the gallery a few weeks ago, that I wasn't doing well. It helps knowing that I am not the only one going through something so difficult. I know it happened to Luca, but he deals with things differently than I do. From what Ryan and Mel tell me, Luca has been burying himself inside of barely legal women—well, girls really—almost every night.

I lie in my bed on this lovely Sunday morning with an emptiness that consumes me. I miss being intimate with someone, but I can't think about intimacy now, at least not until after the baby is born. Realistically, telling a prospective significant other that you are pregnant with your dead husband's baby probably wouldn't sit well with most normal men. On the note of normal men, I have been thinking about Luca a lot lately. I'm not particularly happy about it, but since the day he came in, I can't stop recalling the feeling of need as he stood in front of me.

No matter how hard I try, I see Luca's eyes every time I close mine. I do feel bad for the way I spoke to him, but I couldn't hold it in any longer. When he stepped into the gallery, I felt my heart rip open as thoughts of losing Jake flooded my mind. I also didn't realize the amount of contempt I still hold for Luca. My anxiety gripped me with the strength of a thousand men. My stomach started to knot, and I broke out in a sweat. As the hands of anxiety gripped most of my body, it started to make its way up my throat, making it hard to speak.

I haven't spoken to Luca since then, and that is the way I want to keep it. He doesn't. I know it was a long time ago, but the nagging feeling that I'm not good enough has stayed with me through the years, and nothing will make it go away. I did ask Ryan to keep an eye on him and to keep me posted. Just because I loathe him does not mean I can't be the good person I have always been.

I close my eyes and groan, trying to rid myself of the thought of Luca. I know if I want this baby to be happy—if I want to be happy—I need to get myself together. It has been a rough couple of days. I throw the blankets off me and hop out of bed with a newfound purpose. The hardwood floor is cool, but it feels like the wake-up call I need right now.

I stroll into our master bathroom, and everything seems to be too much without Jake. The white tile floor is cold, but it feels good. I haven't been feeling well, but today is by far the worst of it yet. I figure it is everything sinking in deeper and getting used to all the changes. Today my lower back is sore, and I have some abdominal cramping. If it gets worse, I will call my doctor. The last checkup went well, so I don't let my anxiety get away from me.

Feeling like I have been hit by a truck, I shuffle across the tiles and bend down to turn the gold handles of my shower stall. As the water comes rushing out of the showerhead, I reminisce about how Jake and I used to take baths together every Friday night. It was our way of reacquainting ourselves after we worked all week. I would get home first, usually half an hour before Jake. I would be so excited to have the weekend with him. Sometimes I wouldn't see him much during the week except in the mornings and as I was drifting to sleep. There is also an oversized tub, but I haven't taken a bath since the accident. I can't imagine I would enjoy it now.

I close my eyes and take a deep breath as I fight to keep the food from last night down. I stand up and walk over to the mirror above the double sinks, which covers the entire wall. I open my blue silk robe and let it fall to the floor. Steam covers my view, so I use my right hand to wipe it away. I study myself for a few minutes, wondering what I will look like all fat and pregnant and alone. My hair has gotten longer, and my skin looks radiant. I laugh to myself; pregnancy does look good on me. Tears stain my cheeks, and my heart stops as images of just me and the baby rain on my emotions. Thoughts of getting the nursery ready without Jake make me want to crawl under a rock and never come out. I rub my eyes and force myself to breathe.

My parents moved to Italy after Jake and I married. They had both retired and decided to travel but stopped there for good. They came for the funeral but only stayed for a few days. My dad asked if I wanted them to come back after the baby is born to help me out. I told them not to worry about it now. We will cross that bridge when we get there.

The only people I am still close with are Melanie and Ryan. Ryan is Luca's best friend, and Mel has been my best friend since second grade. We are more like sisters. Neither of us have siblings, but we have each other. We were, and still are, inseparable. If one of us was somewhere, so was the other—until recently. We are complete opposites. Mel is tall with wild red hair and the brightest blue eyes and a slim frame. Guys fall over her wherever she goes, and she never pays attention to them. She is a strong independent woman, never wanting to depend on a man. I think she and Ryan would be great together. Mel is ready for anything life throws her way. She always looked out for me, especially when it came time to deal with Luca. Mel has never liked Luca, and now she has another reason to hate him, even though I remind her he was not even in the car.

Thinking about the accident makes me feel worse. I start to feel more cramping in my abdomen. I keep telling myself if I can just relax, I will feel better. I step into the shower stall and let the warm water relax my muscles. After I wash my hair, I rest my hands on my abdomen, trying to send positive, calm energy to the only connection I have left to Jake, our baby. I already decided on names—Lilly, for a girl, and Nathan, for a boy. I remember when Jake and I talked about kids a couple of years ago, he mentioned he liked both those names.

I am only about three months along, but this baby is the only thing keeping me from completely falling apart. The cramping becomes worse by the minute, but I finish my shower and decide to go to the gallery and clear my head.

*****

When I get to the gallery, I am pleased to find Ann is gone already. She is going out of town for a few days. Just as well, I think. I like being alone more these days than ever before. I don't like running into people; most stare at me in pity. They say they are so sorry and ask if I need anything. I need so much right now, I feel like I don't need a single thing.

I throw my purse on the counter to the right and turn on the lights. There are paintings and some sculptures that arrived early from the participants. These are lying on the floor along the far wall. I have two months to get ready for my next show. There is so much that still has to be done, but I am thankful for the colorful distraction. The show is carnival-themed, with lots of colors and odd amusements. I had asked some of the local sculptors if they would like to be involved in it. Most of the artists I used last time will be coming back for this show as well. It should be fun, of course. It is a twenty-one-years-and-older show.

I am surprised that I still am not feeling well and decide to walk down to Always Brewin' for some chamomile tea. Before I go, I straighten some of the artwork that is strewn across the floor. To get to the bathroom, I step over a pile of carnival-themed binders Ann uses to keep us organized. I shut the door, and I pull down my yoga pants. I sit down to use the toilet and see the blood right away.

*****

Once I check in at the hospital and wait over an hour, I am put in a small room that smells of sickness. I feel like I am losing my mind. I am scared for the baby and myself. I am not sure if I can handle more bad news. I put on the paper-thin gown they give you and slide myself up on the examination table. I wait, barely able to breathe, fidgeting with anything I can get my fingers on. I am still fighting the urge to vomit.

When Dr. Mendez comes in, she gives me a warm smile. She is young, maybe thirty, with long straight black hair. She looks like she is Mediterranean. She is stunning even in her lab coat. I admit that I have always been jealous of women like her who are smart, beautiful, strong, and self-sufficient.

As she examines me, I stare at the ceiling, trying to focus on something other than feeling the worst I have ever felt. I tell her I am almost three months along. She then asks if I am married. I must have tensed my entire body because she stops what she is doing and looks up at me. I clear my throat, whispering that my husband was killed in a car accident about two months ago. She falls silent, and I can see the tears forming in her eyes.

When the exam is finished, she pulls a chair next to me and sits down. I know what she is going to say before the words leave her lips.

"Sunny, I am so sorry to have to tell you this. You are having a miscarriage. It is common in the first trimester and even more common if you've never been pregnant before." As if she knows I am silently blaming myself, she puts her hand on my shoulder. She continues, "It is nothing you did or could have stopped. This is not your fault. Is there anyone I can call for you?"

"No, thank you. Can you give me a few minutes?"

"Sure." Before Dr. Mendez leaves the room, she hands me a business card with a therapist's name and information. "Please talk to someone, Sunny. I know it seems like everything is lost, but you are still here. I'll give you a few minutes to get dressed. I will knock before I come back in." She leaves the room and shuts the door behind her.

I wipe the tears from my face and blow my nose as I take my cell out of my purse and dial Mel. My hands are clumsy with shock, and my vision is blurry from the tears welling up in my eyes.

"Hey, Sun! What's cookin'?" she responds happily.

"So I need you to pick me up from the ER."

"What? Why? Are you okay?" she questions frantically.

"I just need a ride. I'll explain when you get here. Please, Mel," I beg.

"You have the worst timing. I am driving to the conference for the firm. I won't be home until very early Tuesday morning, and I told you about it last week. Sunny, really tell me what's going on. You are freaking me out."

"Shit, I forgot you were going. It's okay. I can find another way home."

"What about Charlotte? What about your assistant, Ann? Ryan will pick you up."

"Charlotte the bartender? I barely know her. Ann is out of town visiting her parents. Ryan is working today, which means Luca is off. I can call Luca."

"Sunny, be serious. Do you trust him at all? Because I don't. He's a fucking pig. Not to mention someone you don't particularly like either. If you must call him, just be careful. He might try to get in your pants. He's gotten worse since Sarah passed. Are you not going to tell me what's going on?"

"You push too much. I had a miscarriage, and I don't feel like crying in the back of some random guy's cab. I need someone familiar right now. I don't think I care who it is." The line goes silent for what seems like forever. "Mel, hello?"

"Oh my god. I am so sorry, Sun. I had no idea you were even pregnant."

"Nobody knew. I only told Jake. I was only about a month before he…" My voice trailed off. "We wanted to wait until I was further along to tell everyone. I really just need to get home."

I know I sound desperate, but I am desperate. Desperate for an embrace only Jake could give. One that makes you forget everything, including yourself.

"Call that jackass and have him get you home. I'll call you as soon as I get back. Should be no later than nine Monday night. Then I'll come over. I love you. Hang in there."

"Sounds good. I love you too, Mel. Be careful."

*****

After I hang up with Mel, I start to text Luca. Then I stop, wondering if he is the right person to ask for a ride. We exchanged numbers that night in case either of us needs anything. *That was his idea*, I remind myself. I was a complete psycho the last time we spoke. I don't know if he will even answer me. Am I asking him because of some weird nonexistent connection to Jake? Do I just need to be near someone I know? Do I want his comfort? Frustrated with myself and all my emotions, I send the text.

> ME. Hey, sorry to bother you, but I need you.
> LUCA. Oh yeah? Never thought you'd admit it…
> ME. Not like that, you ass. I'm at the hospital,
>   and I need a ride home.
> LUCA. You okay?
> ME. No. Can you please just pick me up in front
>   of the ER instead of asking a thousand
>   questions?
> LUCA. Be there in ten. The catch is you have to
>   tell me why you are there or I leave you
>   there.
> ME. Fine.
> LUCA. See you soon.

I throw my phone in my purse, which is sitting on the floor next to me. Then I take off the hospital gown for the exam and throw it in the trash can to my left. I pull on what used to be my favorite yoga pants, T-shirt, and flip-flops. I want to throw them away. My hair is up in a messy bun.

Dr. Mendez knocks and opens the door, and I let her know my ride will be here soon. She tells me to make an appointment with my ob-gyn first thing tomorrow.

I walk out of the exam room and turn into the same hallway I stumbled down not long ago when I was here for Jake. Now I am here for our baby. I rub my eyes, hoping it will clear my head, but I know better. I put my sunglasses on because that's what I need: darkness. I am feeling more alone than I have ever felt. I know I am walking into a world that is now an empty, dark place.

Once outside, I am caught off guard with the feeling of immense relief I feel when I see Luca's black Jeep pull up to the curb where I am waiting.

Luca

Sunny pulls open the passenger side door to climb in. It makes me laugh to myself, how much smaller she is than me as she uses the passenger door to steady herself so she can hop into the passenger seat. To be honest, I am glad she called. I don't like how we left things that day at her gallery. This will, at least, be a start to mending a beyond-burned bridge.

She looks pale and sick, not her usual vibrant self. Her vibrance is reason number 1 of the high school mission "Don't Fall in Love with Sunny." It was hard not to. She is adorable, sweet, and funny. She used to bounce down the halls without a care in the world. Now I can say that it bothered me because I was always under so much pressure to be a certain way. I was jealous. She is very different from anyone I know. Sunny is what people call odd. A complete free spirit who doesn't need anyone's approval, she is one of a kind. I needed someone more polished, more mainstream, which was reason number 2. She was more interested in the arts, and I was into sports. Reason number 3. Looking back, I was just afraid my reputation would be ruined if I admitted how much I wanted her. She fascinates me.

My mom tells me everything happens for a reason. *What? No.* I can't think about this anymore. I am picking Sunny up from the hospital after we both buried our spouses, and all I can think about is how not to fall for her. Not that I would mind if she would let me touch her. That would be nice too. *Stop. Stop. Stop.* Even for me, this is bad. Sunny has that effect on me. She always did, and I hate it. The sound of the door slamming shut brings me out of my daydream.

Sunny wipes her cheeks and forces her lips to smile. She is an absolute mess, her hair piled on top of her head, completely disheveled. Her hands nervously move up and down the tops of her thighs. She thanks me for getting here so fast.

"Aren't you glad I suggested exchanging numbers?" I point out.

She agrees then takes her attention off me and places it somewhere far beyond the car window. Normally, I don't pressure someone into telling me things they don't want to, but she did call me. I am intrigued. Before I can ask her if she is okay, she mumbles about how she is sorry for the way she spoke to me when I went to her gallery.

"No need to apologize. I'm sure I deserved much more than what you said."

I can see her lips give way to a small smile that looks like it catches her off guard. I am enjoying this—maybe too much. I relish how she seems she still wants to hate me, but I know she needs someone to comfort her. I am more than up to the challenge. I wonder why she didn't call Mel. I feel myself become aroused as my thoughts run wild, wondering why she chose me. And once again, I almost forget something bad had to have happened to her today, and I still don't know what it is.

She takes a deep breath and looks away. She is afraid to let me in. Her voice sounds as though something invisible is trying to suffocate her. I know this is going to be bad. Her hands still rub the tops of her thighs, now with more vigor as her hands shake uncontrollably. She is struggling to get out what brought her here. Finally, she explains she suffered a miscarriage. Her words shatter my heart. I see tears falling under her sunglasses when she asks me to take her home so she can drown her sorrows.

I stare at her in shock, but she is lost in the news she just received. Is there anything I can say? How would I have reacted if they told me Sarah was pregnant? Staring at her in disbelief and feeling like there is nothing I can do, I put my hand on hers and tell her, "I can help with drowning sorrows. I'm good at that." I take my foot off the brake and head to Hounds, the local bar.

When we get to Hounds, I feel a calm wash over me. It is a one-story brick front painted white with a large green front door that says "Must Be 21 To Enter" on the tinted window. Two slender horizontal windows are on either side of the main entrance. One reads BEER, the other HAPPY HOUR. Each has a light above it. The green awning on top of the building reads Hounds Bar in large white letters.

I pull into a close parking spot and turn the Jeep off. I turn to her, but she won't meet my eyes. She looks like a space cadet. "You want anything to eat?"

She shakes her head no. I get out and walk to the front door.

I pull the heavy door open, and the smell of alcohol and too much perfume invade my nostrils. That smell is soaked into the wood floors. The inside has dim lighting, somehow making the smell more potent. I walk past the pool tables on the left, making my way to the bar. I see my buddy, Ryan, is already there. He is talking to the cute blonde behind the bar.

Lately, we have worked opposite shifts, so I haven't seen him much. He is the kind of guy that can make you laugh no matter your mood. Although I have withdrawn from society on some level, Ryan is the person that I stay in consistent contact with. I have appreciated him using his sense of humor to help me. However, the nightly visits I get from the barely legal all-too-eager girls ease some of my sufferings.

"Ry, it's three in the afternoon. You here already? Thought you were working today," I tease, putting my hand on his shoulder.

"Yo, Monts," Ryan bellows. "I got done at seven this morning. Let me buy you a beer or five. You look like you need ten," he jokes as I take a seat next to him at the bar.

"Thanks, Ry, but I have Sunny waiting outside."

"I'm sorry. Say again? Sunny? She let you talk her into getting in the same car as you?"

"Hilarious. She contacted me."

"Why? Was she feeling lonely, so she needed you to help her out?"

"Shut the fuck up, man." I laugh as I smack him upside the head.

"Hey, Charlotte, bring your pretty face over here. I need to order some food to go," I yell to the bartender.

Charlotte is cute. I'm pretty sure our buddy, Jimmy, has a crush on her. Her hair is dark blond and made of huge loose curls that dust her shoulders. Her eyes are the most interesting shade of green, her smile wide and ever-present. She is small, but you can tell she can hold her own.

Her job is not just as a bartender. She thinks it is also her job to tell me what I need right now. I tell her I am how I am. I can take a barely legal girl home for a one-night stand every night if I want to. After that, she starts telling me which crazy ones to stay away from. She tries getting the barely legal drinkers that frequent the bar to pick me up so I don't destroy some eighteen-year-old. It's funny in a way. I flirt and humor Charlotte, but we never get too far.

"Well, if it isn't Luca Claymont. Hey, doll." She bends over the bar for a cheek kiss. I oblige. She is sweet and keeps me in line if I drink too much. "What can I get you from the kitchen, hon?"

"I need a bacon cheeseburger well done and a Rueben, as fast as you can. I'll also need two bottles of Pinot Grigio and a bottle of your best scotch."

"Coming right up." Charlotte flashes her big smile and disappears behind the swinging door to the kitchen.

"Ryan, stop looking at me like that." I don't need to look to know he is staring at me.

"Sorry, man. She called you? I really can't wrap my head around that." His tone is complete disbelief.

"She texted me. She needed some help." I try to sound as uncaring as I can. Ryan knows me well enough to know I care. "She probably thought you were still at work."

"I gave her my schedule, but I'm sure she didn't memorize it. Want to share? I need something else to focus on. The drama at the firehouse has been ridiculous. A bunch of damn women over there. I hate the night shift," he complains.

"Nope. I am, however, going to grab our food and booze and get back to Sunny."

Charlotte comes over from the kitchen holding two bags, and she hands them to me.

"Thanks, Char." I stand up, pay, and give Ryan a few pats on the back. "See you, guys."

*****

I was only in the bar for twenty minutes, but when I open the driver's side door, I see Sunny sleeping. Her head rests against the window; her breathing is calm and even. She looks at peace. Seeing her like this kills me inside. I keep telling myself it is because I know the pain of losing someone the way she does. I think I am handling things just fine, but she is not. I push away the thought that says it is because I love her and I always have. It's crazy. I'm not that guy.

I slide the bags onto the back seat and close the door as quietly as I can so I don't wake her. I can smell her lavender shampoo; it fills my Jeep. The smell punches me in the gut like a heavyweight drops his opponent. I didn't smell it as much when she first got in, but now I want to smell lavender all day and all night.

I pull out of the lot and drive down Magnolia Boulevard and up the only hill in town to Tulston Street. Her house is large. I thought she would have more of a cottage-type house. We get up to her house and pull into the long driveway. I shut the car off and lightly touch her cheek. Her skin is pale but warm to the touch.

Her body jumps, and her head jerks up. She gasps for air. "I'm sorry," she whispers.

"Don't apologize. You are home. We stopped at Hounds, and I picked us up some food and alcohol. Thought we could both use a break from reality, at least for a little while. We have earned it, no?"

She turns to me and smiles. She smiled *at* me for the first time. I want more. I want her to laugh and run her thin fingers down my face. I know it will be a long time before that happens. I am willing to work for her trust. I owe it to her. At least, that's what I keep telling myself.

We get out and slowly walk up the brick path to the front door. She unlocks it, and I push it open for her. I am having a hard time seeing her like this: broken. This is not her, and I want—no, need—to help her.

She leads me into a spacious living room with beige walls and dark polished hardwood flooring. Sheer white curtains clothe the large windows that make up the back and front walls, showcasing the ongoing yard and professional landscaping. I follow her to the kitchen, passing a cluster of seating choices on a white area rug held in place by the glass coffee table in the middle. I never pictured Sunny, the free-thinking artist who bought an art gallery, would live in a house like this.

"Your house is breathtaking, big. For two people."

"Thanks. Jake was a lawyer, and we were planning on having a few kids." She points to the black marble counter. "You can put that stuff there. What did you get?"

"I got you a bacon cheeseburger and fries. You look a little pale. And I got a Reuben. I also got you some white wine and a bottle of scotch for myself."

She looks shocked that I got her something even though she said she wasn't hungry. *That's right, Sunny. I'm not that bad. You will see.*

"Good call on everything." She looks at me in confusion, as though I never gave her a second thought. She never knew how much attention I paid to her.

"You're welcome." I smile.

I sit at the island in the center of the kitchen while she grabs a couple of glasses from the cabinet to the left of the sink. She turns, walks over, and sits across from me. I open the wine, then my scotch, and pour us each a drink as she intently watches my every move.

I raise my scotch and Sunny her wine. "To new beginnings," I contend.

"To new beginnings, no matter how odd they may be." She clinks my glass and finishes her wine in two gulps. She holds the empty glass in front of my face with a devilish smile that ignited something inside me.

"Can I do something for you?" I tease.

"My glass is empty. You are supposed to be taking care of me today," she explains, sliding her glass in front of me.

"Uh-huh. Is that the deal for today?" The thought of being with her for more than a few minutes, no less taking care of her, bring on feelings that I thought I destroyed long ago. I did like the thought of taking care of her. Maybe it will take away some of the guilt I've been carrying. I grab the open bottle of wine and do as she asks.

"Thank you." She smiles again.

She is wearing one of those oversized shirts that fall off her shoulder, just loose enough in the front to get a decent peek. I can't help but stare. Her breasts are full, and she turns me on.

I quickly shift my focus on unwrapping my sandwich, and I try to stop my feelings from causing a scene. It sure as hell is not the day for that.

We sit in silence for a while, eating, drinking, and trying to be comfortable.

Sunny

I sit across from Luca, amused, as he fumbles with the wrapper on his sandwich. He looks like a kid who got caught looking through the window of the girl next door, trying to pretend he was doing something else. He is different today. He got me food and wine even though I told him I wasn't hungry. He is being overly nice, and I have no idea why. I am not going to question him either. He did me a favor today, and I feel like I owe him as much not to question his motives. I finish my second glass, and Luca refills it before I can ask.

I let out a groan as I bite into the juicy burger in front of me. I didn't realize how hungry I am. Hounds is the best spot in town for food. They beat out everyone on restaurant row, which stretches down Marvin Drive, for the best small-town eatery. Although the Lovely Italian is a very close second, and Maria's Diner is the best for breakfast after a long night. I love Rolling Hills, even if there was only one hill in town. The mayor had the roads of the town square redone with cobblestone; it added more charm. The square had grown quite a bit in the last few years. It was on the up and up, as some would say.

"Thank you for everything you did for me today." I look at him, but this time, he surprises me.

"I thought I was supposed to take care of you today. It isn't dark yet, is it?"

"I didn't know if you had somewhere else to be, like balls deep inside an eighteen-year-old," I prod.

His eyes soften. "I'd rather be making sure you get through tonight."

I can smell his cologne from here, and it is comforting. I miss smelling a man around the house. Sometimes I spray my pillow with Jake's just to feel close to him.

"Oh, are you spending the night?" I hold his gaze and lift one of my eyebrows.

"Slow down, girl." He grins. "I would be more than happy to do things to—"

"Stop." I feel my cheeks burn, and my heart just about stops. I can't say I never thought about it, but I'm not even close to drunk enough to do anything with him. And today—seriously? Of all days. The bleeding has stopped, but it's probably not smart either way. Why am I even thinking about this? I just lost the rest of my world. I conclude it is just my sick way of coping with everything that has happened. A warm, strong body holding me sounds like exactly what I need, but I am not going to let him know that. "I'm not like you. I can't just use someone," I said, half joking.

"Is this the thanks I get? Damn, Sun. You better beg me to stay or I'm out." He laughs.

"Ha ha. I am exhausted. I think I'm going to change and lie down. Are you hanging out?"

"I was going to. Is Mel coming over?"

"No, she is on her way to a work conference. She won't be back until Tuesday. I need to make a doctor's appointment for tomorrow morning."

"I can stay if you don't want to be alone, and I can take you to your appointment so that you have some support. You okay with that?"

"Why are you doing all this?"

"I'm in a good mood." He winks.

I excuse myself to call and make the appointment, forgetting it is Sunday. A happy young voice answers, and I let out a sigh of relief. I tell the receptionist what happened, and she tells me to come first thing in the morning. She apologizes and says I should call if I need anything.

I can't get over what is going on. I usually don't drink, so after a few glasses of wine, my head could be messing with me. Is he honestly being this nice? Why am I so surprised? Do I miss having someone so much, I am willing to let Luca stay here? Maybe this is a bad idea. Maybe it isn't. I need to lie down. I should trash these clothes first.

After we finish eating, I clean up the remnants of our meal. I can feel Luca's eyes on me, and I don't hate it. I turn and prop myself against the counter and ask if he wants to see the rest of the house. I take him through the rest of the downstairs, then he follows me upstairs. He comments on some of my art pieces that line the hallway. I start feeling better that he is going to stay. I'm not so nervous anymore.

We get to my bedroom, and he follows closely behind me. I can feel the heat coming off him, and I can feel his rough hands grab my waist. He probably thinks I'm going to fall over from the wine. That's what I'm telling myself anyway.

"I am going to take a shower. Do you want to hang in here or downstairs? There is a TV along the far wall. You can do whatever. Make yourself comfy." I really shouldn't be inviting the devil to stay anywhere near me, but the words fall out of my mouth before I can stop them. *Damn wine.*

Luca smiles and makes himself comfortable on my bed.

"Do you need help getting in?" he teases like he is expecting me to say yes.

His smile is evil, and I can't decide if I am turned on or angry that he is being so insensitive right now. I walk toward the bathroom and tell him I am fine, but it feels like my body is on fire.

I shut the door and hear the bedroom TV turn on. I look in the mirror, seeing a much different reflection than this morning. Now I am alone. I no longer have a husband or a baby, just a big empty house. My face has no color except for my cheeks that are burning with every emotion possible. I am waiting to self-combust, but to my disappointment, it doesn't happen. I think if I run a bath, I will be able to wash away my feelings enough to pass out for a while. I wonder if I can ask him to lie with me without him being ridiculous. I haven't slept, and I have concluded it is because I hate sleeping alone and nothing else.

I can't calm my mind no matter how hard I try. I have handled a lot of challenging situations in my life. I will get through this too. Turning the water as hot as I can stand, I peel my clothes off and let them fall to the floor. As I step into the shelter of the water, I feel myself become weak, so I sit on the shower floor and fall apart.

After a half hour, I decide I need some sleep. I shut the water off and hurry to get dressed and forget today. To my surprise, when I open the door, Luca is resting comfortably in my bed. He opens his eyes and props himself up.

"Feel better?" he inquires as he starts to get up.

"A little. Y-you don't have to, um, get up if you are comfortable," I stammer.

"Oh? Maybe I won't. Your couch doesn't look this inviting. I think I deserve a good night's sleep. Unless you are just being sweet."

"No. Actually, I am being selfish for once. I haven't slept well in so long, and I just don't want to be alone right now," I explain.

"I guess after everything you've been through, I could stay here while you fall asleep," he offers, pulling the sheets down next to him. "Come on. You look exhausted."

I do as he says, not caring or feeling anything. My limbs are heavy as I lie on my side next to him. He turns the light off and slides closely behind me, pulling me close to him. My phone buzzes incessantly on the night table closest to Luca and I groan. I ask if he can see if it is someone important because I don't feel like talking to anyone. He tells me it is Mel and asks if I want him to answer. I am relieved that he would do that for me, so I nod my head.

He turns on the lamp next to him and answers. I hear Mel yelling on the other end about why he is answering my phone so late and why the hell he is still here. I hear her as clearly as if I am holding the phone.

I roll over to face him and mouth, "I'm so sorry."

He gives me the greatest smile. Is that the smile everyone else sees? Is this sweet person who he is? I need not fool myself. I know it's just because I need him right now, that's all.

He convinces Mel he is taking care of me and that she doesn't need to worry. He gently insists that she get some sleep, and he will have me call in the morning after my appointment. I'm surprised by how turned on I become when he takes control of a situation—impressed or tipsy, not sure which.

Luca hangs up, turns the light off, and slides back to his spot behind me. His arm is back to its place around my waist. And as he pulls me to him, I can feel him getting aroused, but I am too tired to say anything and too comfortable. My eyes close, and for the first time in months, I drift off within seconds.

Luca

I wake up the next morning to an overcast sky and Sunny trying to sneak out of bed without waking me. I don't know what to think about last night, but for now, I am only worried about getting her through the next few hours. When I check my phone, I see it is seven thirty. Sunny slides out from my grip as she sniffles and lets her hair cover her face as she hurries to the bathroom. Sunny said she doesn't drink much, but last night, she drank like it was her job. Not that I blame her. I will see how she feels after the appointment, but I am going to insist I stay with her until Mel gets back. Last night wasn't great, and tonight probably won't be any better. Maybe worse.

Around eight fifteen, she emerges from the bathroom, her hair in a perfect bun with soft curls falling around her shoulders. Her eyes are made up to cover the emotions of last night and the tiredness left on her face. I smile at her and get up to head to the bathroom so we can get this nightmare underway.

"You will be okay. I am not going to leave you," I assure her, her beautiful face cradled in my hand for a moment as I pass her to wash off the sexual frustration that is heavy on my mind.

Twenty minutes later, we are in the Jeep and on our way. I hope the rain holds out until we are back at her place. She is quiet the whole way, except for her periodic sniffles. Pulling into a parking spot near the entrance of the doctor's office, I can feel the rest of Sunny's heart break.

After I turn the engine off, I shift in my seat to face Sunny. Space has her enveloped in a dangerous grip. She jumps when I put my hand over hers. "You ready?" I know she isn't. "I will be in the waiting room for you.

When you are done, we can stop for food and restock on the alcohol. I won't leave you alone. I promise."

She smiled with tears in her eyes and replied with a simple thank-you.

I jump out of the Jeep and open her door, helping her out. I grab her hand, offering support as we go inside. I swing the door open and step aside so Sunny can go in first. I follow her, and as soon as I walk in, the receptionist steals my attention. I'd notice her anywhere. *Sassy.* Of all places this psycho has to work. I have been dodging her messages apologizing for the vases she broke and how she reacted. Honestly, she never had a chance, and it's past time I put my foot down with her.

A bubbly young woman calls Sunny back, and I decide to take this time to smoke an occasional cigarette. I usually don't smoke, but I don't want to have to deal with Sassy's evil stares. I head out and let the warm air melt my cold side, which has been out since I laid eyes on Psycho Sassy. Lighting my cigarette, I can hear the door open behind me.

"Mind if I smoke with you?" Sassy interrupts.

"I suppose," I snap coldly.

"Listen. I just wanted to tell you I am sorry about breaking that stuff at your house, but I needed you to understand how hurt I was. I mean, it was pretty fucked up of you to call me a cab." She continues, "Then you show up here with a pregnant woman who lost her husband. What the hell is with you?"

I take a long drag off my cigarette, trying to calm myself before I answer her. I don't want to make a scene. "Look, I don't have time for this. You are nothing but drama, and I am not into it. You break shit leaving my house then you expect me to answer you. Are you hoping I will ask you out again? Please get those thoughts out of your head. I cannot deal with a little girl with an unhealthy crush. As you can see, I am dealing with something much more serious at the moment, and I don't need you to make my life more complicated. You have to stop messaging me." With that, I threw my cigarette to the ground and put it out with my shoe. "Now if you'll excuse me, I have a friend to take care of."

"Did you get her pregnant? Did you abandon her when she needed you?" Sassy growled.

"Look, you little bitch. I don't need to explain shit to you. Stay away from me, stop messaging me, and damnit. If you bother Sunny, so help me God. I am going back in there to wait for her. When you get back to your desk, act like I'm not here," I bark as I stomp past her and back inside to wait for Sunny.

About forty-five minutes later, Sunny appears from the back. Her eyes are red and puffy. It's going to be a long day.

I help Sunny into the Jeep and strap her in. Her body is weighed down by sadness, and her mind is trying to wrap her head around all this loss. She doesn't say a word on the way back, but the raindrops hitting my windshield turn the deafening silence down.

I pull into the diner parking lot and run inside to get the food I called in after we left the doctor's office. It smells incredible, as usual. I run back to my car and toss the bag of food onto Sunny's lap.

"I could go for a few strong mimosas," she states.

"I hate to disappoint you, but how strong can a mimosa be?" I joke.

"Ha ha ha."

*****

After dinner, we decide to have a few more drinks. We watch a stupid comedy, and we can't stop laughing.

"Luca, I'm tired. Can we call it a night?"

"Anything you want. Let me help your drunk ass up the stairs."

She looks at me and smiles.

Her bedroom is nice, like a master suite in a penthouse. The bed is comfortable (as I found out last night) and feels good after today's events. I am feeling the scotch, and it feels good. I flick on the TV but turn the volume down until, finally, I hear the water filling the tub. Most women I've met are overemotional, but I can't imagine what she is dealing with right now. First Jake and now this. Hopefully, she doesn't try to drown herself. I don't need that shit on my conscience. Not after having to deal with Sassy earlier.

I hear faint sniffles coming from the bathroom, so I get up and quietly walk over to the bathroom door and put my ear against it. It is Sunny trying to cover up her quiet sobs. I feel horrible, and she is broken, more broken than over anything I ever said to her. I knock on the door.

Nothing.

I knock again. "Sun, are you okay?"

"I'm fine," she whimpers.

"Is the door locked?"

"No."

"I'm coming in."

She doesn't say anything. I open the door, and she is wrapped in a pink towel and lying on her left side on the floor. Her eyes are puffy, her face red from crying, and she looks like she blew her nose a thousand times. She doesn't look at me. She is looking to a place that exists beyond her mess of a bathroom. I step around her and turn the water off before the tub overflows and her bath is ruined.

I sit on the cold floor behind her and pull her hair out of the elastic she has it tied in. Her long curls tumble to the floor, releasing another round of lavender that I have become addicted to. I run my left hand through her hair, letting the softness swallow my rough skin, while my right hand rests heavily on her shoulder. I have no clue what to do, so I sit her up and turn her to face me. She looks through me as though I don't exist.

Fuck.

What do I do?

She is not okay, and I am the only one here to help her.

Get her into the water.

That was all she wanted to do. Help her into the tub.

I stand up and then bend down. I put one hand under her legs and the other behind her back and scoop her off the floor. She is tiny to begin with, but I don't believe she has eaten much lately. She puts her arms around my neck and her head on my shoulder. When I get her over the tub, I lean close to her ear and ask her if she wants to keep her towel on, but she doesn't answer. She just stares through me. She looks like she is strung out. I know she isn't, but she deserves to be out of it. I only see one towel hanging on the hook, so I stand her up in front of me and I unwrap her. I am careful not to look at her even though that is all I want to do. I pick her back up and gently place her in the warm water. I can't deny it looks soothing—not that I am one for bubble baths.

Her body slips under the blanket of bubbles. She puts her head against the wall and closes her eyes. She is sexy as hell completely covered in bubbles. Drops of water make her skin shimmer. A vulnerability was never something she showed, but now that I see it, I like it.

"Feel a little better?" I sit back down on the floor next to the tub. I know I can't leave her in there by herself.

"Thank you," she answers, trying not to choke on her tears. She turns to look at me. "You look like you need a bubble bath too." She laughs.

"Is that an invite?" I know it is a long shot, and she probably thinks I am heartless. I have concluded that I care about what happens to Sunny because we share something that no one our age should go through. *No other reason*, I muse, trying to convince myself. Then the unthinkable happens.

"Two conditions," she clarifies, choosing her words carefully.

"They are?" I can't wrap my head around what is going on, but I don't question her.

"One, say yes when I ask you to spend the night—strictly so I can get a good night's sleep. I haven't slept well by myself. Two, no playing with things you shouldn't be playing with. For example, me."

"Can I trust you not to play with me?" I raise my brow at her, and she rolls her eyes.

I do get a small smile out of her. If there is one thing I've learned, it's that sad women like to be comforted. Any way they can get it, they will take it. For Sunny, I'll be a good boy. For now.

I take my clothes off in front of her, catching her as she stares. I can't help feeling my confidence soar higher than ever. She scoots forward so I can sit behind her. This tub is big enough for two more people. I sit against the wall, grab her by the waist with my left arm, and pull her close with her back to my chest. Her skin feels like silk, but her muscles are tense. I wrap my legs around her and try to get her to relax.

She takes a deep breath, and her chin quivers as she tries not to start crying again. She puts her head on my chest and closes her eyes. I gather water in my right hand and run it over her hair and just hold her. I want to do more, but I keep thinking about fat naked grandmas outside on a hot day so I don't scare her. Besides, she needs to trust me before all that happens.

Sunny

I have no idea why I let him in my tub. Probably because I need him to stay the night. I need some sleep. What I never realized is how much I love having a man in the house. He has done nothing to make me think he would be a jerk, he has taken me to the doctor, so I should give him the benefit of the doubt. Right now, I welcome any soothing touch, even if it's his.

We soak in the comfort of the water. His body is muscular, anchoring me to reality. He is holding me around my waist with his left arm while he uses his right hand to soak my hair with water. It feels as though he gives a shit if I am okay. I am so relaxed toward the end, I almost fall asleep on him. The water starts to cool down, and he flips the drain with his foot, the noise insisting I open my eyes.

He gets out first and grabs a towel from the hook on the wall and wraps it around his waist. His pecs are massive, and his abs look like they have been chiseled from stone. He is not shy, that is for sure—not that he has any reason to be. He steps back over and holds another towel in front of me, and he looks away while I stand up and take the towel from him. The softness warms me. He then picks me up out of the tub and stands me on the floor.

"Shame you are a fan of towels." The low grumble of his voice is like an aphrodisiac.

"Well, I'll be wearing more than a towel to bed. Behave yourself, please. I need you to stay so I can sleep," I beg.

He puts his arms around my waist and focuses on my eyes. "I promise I will do nothing but hold you while you fall asleep. You cannot hold me responsible if my body decides to react to yours and it touches you with no encouragement on my part. Sometimes that happens to guys, you know."

"Ass." I can't help but smile as I push against his chest, and he breaks his oddly tight grip on me. I know he is just trying to make me feel better.

He clutches my hand and leads me toward my bed without stopping so I can grab my pajamas. We are still just wearing towels. Once we reach the side of the bed, he stands aside, lifting one side of the sheet and comforter, and he signals for me to lie down. I am too tired to argue. He climbs in behind me and covers us both after turning the light off. He puts his arm around my waist, as if to keep me from floating away as we fall into the comfort of each other. His body is warm as he tucks me into his embrace. I can hear his heart beating—a soothing rhythm my mind clings to. I close my eyes and decide to let my body melt under the safety of a man I have hated for so long.

*****

The next morning, I wake up with a killer headache. The curtains are not closed, and the sun coming through the window is blinding at first. I feel like my skull has been cracked open with a crowbar. I don't remember much except that I drank too much. I feel a heavy arm on my side, and my stomach jumps into my throat. I am wearing nothing. The towel I had on came undone while I was asleep.

What did I do?

Why is he still here?

Fuck. Fuck. Fuck.

What the hell was I thinking?

I turn over to face him, and he opens his eyes and smiles. His dimples are deep, and for once, his eyes don't look sinister. He isn't wearing a shirt, but I can't remember if he had anything on when we crawled into my bed last night. I try to push the thought of him naked in my bed away, but all I feel is want between my legs. I can't remember much of anything, just bits and pieces. *This is why I don't drink.*

"Good morning. How do you feel today?" He strokes my hair, looking into my soul.

"I'm not sure. My head is killing me. Did we…?"

"No, Sun, nothing happened. We ate, we drank, you cried a lot, and we took a relaxing bubble bath."

"We took a bath?" I raise my brow. He makes me nervous, so self-conscious.

"We did."

The evil smile and sinister eyes have made their appearance. I knew it wouldn't last long.

"So you saw me?" My cheeks burn, and my hands start to sweat. I can feel a lump form in my throat, threatening to make me sick. He never made me feel good about myself, just bad. Always bad.

"Relax. Believe it or not, I was a gentleman. And there were so many bubbles, I couldn't see if I tried. Which I didn't, and it wasn't easy, you know. Then you asked me to stay over because you hadn't slept in so long," he explains with an innocence I can't deny.

I still don't trust him. He tore me apart so long ago, and those scars have not faded much.

"So," he continues, "what happened to the towel you were wrapped in?" His eyes start to wander, and his hand is about to lift the sheet.

"Don't you dare," I sternly warn him, smacking his hand before he touches the edge.

"Okay. Okay. I'm just messing with you. You need to laugh a little." He throws his hands up in surrender. With that, he whips the covers off himself and gets up. The towel he was wearing is still in the bed. Not a care in the world, not that I mind the distraction.

When he comes back out, he can see I am a mess. He rushes over to me, grabs his jeans, pulls them on, and sits next to me on the edge of the bed. He takes my hand in his and starts rubbing it between his thumb and forefinger. He looks so concerned, but I can't trust him. I wish I could. I can't trust my judgment, so how can I trust someone else?

"You have to go. Thank you for taking care of me, but you have to leave. Now." I can't look at him. My throat is strangled with anxiety.

"Are you fucking kidding me? What's wrong? Why are you so upset?" His face twisted, and his eyes grew dark. He looks genuinely hurt. I am such an asshole.

"I'm so sorry, but I don't trust you. And I need to process what happened to me the last few days."

"You do know I was there for you and didn't leave you. I even thought about fat naked grandmas most of the night so I didn't get turned on by you, and you don't trust me. Sunny, please don't shut me out. Do you know people our age who have lost their spouse have a high suicide rate in the first year after it happens? We can be there for each other. Why are you having such a hard time with this?" he pleads.

I pull my hand from him. "Two days of you doing something decent does not make me trust you. I do appreciate what you did for me, but… I'm sorry. I need you to go."

I don't want him to go, but I can't have him taking baths with me, making me feel safe. That isn't Luca; it never was.

He gets up, puts his shirt on, and grabs his sneakers. He won't look at me as he storms out of my bedroom and down the stairs. I jump when the front door slamming shut sounds like that of betrayal, and then I watch him pull away.

I call Mel to come over and have lunch. I don't want company, but I also know I shouldn't be alone.

Sunny

Mel blows through my front door like a tornado. She looks like her head is going to explode. Her red hair looks like a California wildfire, and the tapping of her stilettos sounds like a gavel that is being wielded by a judge trying to make themselves seem more important than they are. We sit in the kitchen, where Luca and I had been yesterday. If I am being honest with myself, I wish Luca were sitting here now. I can't explain how I feel or why, but I am tired of trying to understand things. Nothing has made sense in months, so why should this? Besides, my head is throbbing, and I can feel my temples pulsating.

Mel is babbling on about how he never should have stepped foot in my door. She can't understand what his motive is. I try to tell her I didn't think he had one. I needed someone, and he knew that. I also reminded her that Luca and I share something that will connect us forever no matter how much we try to deny it.

"I honestly just don't get it, Sun. He got you drunk and decided it was a good idea to get you in a bubble bath with him. I'm sorry, but what the hell were you thinking?" She looks at me like a disappointed parent looking at a delinquent kid.

"Mel, I love you, but you don't understand." I am enraged that she would dwell on this instead of helping me. "My parents are in Italy, you were not around, Ryan was working, and I needed someone. I didn't care who it was. I lost my only connection to Jake, our baby. I am a fucking mess. I can say, I don't know if I would have made it through the night if it wasn't for Luca. He made it okay for a little while. Then I kicked him out this morning because I realized I can't get too comfortable with him just because he is being nice for one night.

And by the way, the bath was my idea. I didn't intend on him being in there with me, but it was comforting," I rant.

I am more irritated with her than I want to be. I take a breath and drop my head in my hands and start to cry again. When I look back at her, she has a look of pity in her eyes.

"I'm sorry, my Sun. You are right. I can't imagine what you are going through. I just know how he is, and that is not what you need right now. How are you feeling?"

"Better today aside from the wine headache." I smile.

We talk for a couple of hours over food. I start to feel better as the day goes on. Mel was always good for lifting spirits.

We move to the living room and flop on my oversized couch. Everything in this house seems oversized now. I lie on the couch with my head on Mel's lap, and she strokes my head. We decide to watch action movies because I just couldn't handle any chick flicks. When I wake up a few hours later, I realize she has put a blanket over me and left.

Luca

Ryan corners me at work on Friday to talk about what happened at Sunny's last week. He doesn't seem angry, so I don't know if he already spoke to Sunny and Mel. It's not like I did anything wrong. We sit at the table in the kitchen, and I explain what happened to Sunny and why I was with her that day. I disclose the details of what I still think to be the night we connected for the first time. No judgment on either end, just comfort, knowing we can move on from the past. But supposedly, it isn't that simple.

Ryan is quiet for a minute, making me feel like I did something I shouldn't have. He asks what happened next. I finish the story from that night, and he nods his head. He reveals he has spoken to Mel the day after and Sunny the day after that. He notes that Sunny and I conveyed the same thing, but when he spoke to Mel, she was freaking out.

"Dude, Mel swears you two are hiding something, and she refuses to let it go," Ryan warns.

I put my arms on the table and lean toward Ryan, lowering my voice, "Ry, I confess I can't get Sun out of my head. Every time I close my eyes, I envision her in her tub. Knowing she doesn't trust me hurts more than I am comfortable with. I need serious help. This is not good."

Ryan leans back in his chair, entertained by what I just said. His hands are on his lap, a grin fills his face, and his pale skin turns pink. "I knew it. You have not talked about anyone aside from her. Have you gone about business as usual—ya know, the young ones?"

I sit back and cross my arms in front of my chest, not wanting to admit Sunny has this effect on me. Ryan knows me the best, and if he sees something, I am not being as cautious about my emotions as I had hoped. I stay silent. "Uh-huh." He chuckles.

"I am only telling you this because you are my best friend and the voice of reason. Lay it on me. I need Ryan's advice right now."

"You want my advice." He sits up and puts his forearms on the table. "You need to do whatever it takes to get her to trust you. Go see her show coming up in a couple of months. Stop by the gallery to say hello. Ask her out for dinner. Come on. You act as if you have never dated anyone," he blurts out. "Seriously though." Ryan leans in with his finger pointed at me. "Leave the sympathy squad alone! Have you slept with any of them lately?"

Ryan's question stuns me because I can't lie to him, and I wasn't trying to let this tidbit out. His chair slams forward and makes a loud noise. Drawing in a deep breath and narrowing his eyes, he says accusingly, "Luca, what did you do this time?"

I take just enough time to realize he will find out anyway. "It's Sassy."

"What's Sassy? She's way off, man," he warns.

I let out a grunt. "I got her pregnant."

"You what?" Ryan stares at me like I just broke his heart. "What if Sunny finds out? What is Sassy doing about the baby?"

"No, Sunny does not know. Nor does she need to. Sassy was before her," I explain. "Besides, I took her to get an abortion as soon as she told me. Best decision I have ever made. That mess never would have cut it as a mother."

"I don't get it. Luca, you have been my friend since we were kids. But when it comes to women, I just don't get how you are a complete dick, and they keep coming back for more. I can't even get the nerve to call Mel and see if she wants to get together and possibly go to Sunny's show as my date."

I chuckle because it's true. "To answer your original question, no. I have not answered one sympathy message in a while because of Sassy and that drama. Honestly, when it comes to Sunny, I feel like an idiot. It's like she flips a switch in me, keeping me from thinking clearly. I wonder if this is how she feels when I am around," I question. "Whatever I figure out, I don't want to wait until her next show. It's too far away."

At this point, I move on from what used to be between Sunny and me to what I am going to do now. For the rest of my shift, this is all that is on my mind.

Sunny

My eyes are heavy when I wake up on Friday morning. My head is still foggy from the past week, and I have been at the gallery every day from six in the morning, sometimes until midnight. It is exhausting, but I am happy to be out of the house and around my assistant, Ann.

Ann is in her midforties and is not married. She affirms she does what she is passionate about, not what society expects of her. Maybe that is why I enjoy her company as much as I have grown to. Ann judges no one and has the heart of a saint. Since my miscarriage, she has been sending me home with so much food, I am not sure what to do with it. As of today, I still have four platters of food in my freezer. She apologizes every day that she was not here when it happened, but I keep telling her no one could have known.

Once again, feelings of regret over how I spoke to Luca get me thinking as to how I can say I'm sorry. I kick the blankets off and head to the bathroom, where I shower and brush my teeth. I walk back into the bedroom and open my walk-in closet. I have been wearing nothing more than yoga pants and tank tops, but today I feel the need to at least look as though I am human. I search for something cute but comfortable. I have work to do today. I come across a black summer dress with white flowers. This was Jake's favorite. I toss it on over my head and pull it down so it is comfortable. When I look in the mirror, I am pleased to see I don't look as much like death. Perfect. I have to see what I need from the store.

I go downstairs and almost sprint to the kitchen. Realizing that this is making me happy, I am sure this will work. I scour my cabinets and the refrigerator only to learn I have nothing I need. I fetch a pen and a piece of paper from the magnetic hanging basket to the left of the fridge. Flour, eggs, vanilla extract, baking powder, butter, and cream. The only ingredient I do have is sugar. Imagine that. I get my things and head out.

It takes me two hours to get to the grocery store in the next town and back. Fridays are terrible for traffic around here. The store isn't too crowded, and I can get everything I need and even a few things I don't. I haven't cooked or baked anything in months, and I am looking forward to my afternoon of kitchen craziness. I love to bake, and the apology to Luca is a good reason to start again.

Finally home, I rush to the kitchen and place my groceries on the island and unpack everything. I take mixing bowls out of the cabinet to the far right and mixing utensils from the drawer below it. I mix and crack and mix some more until the batter is ready. I line the cupcake pan with paper wrapping and pour the vanilla mixture, careful not to waste anything.

For Luca, I am making a mini cake that looks like a bubble bath. The cake is vanilla with blue food coloring for the water. Then I will use vanilla icing to cover the cake, but on top, there will be a shallow square cut out so that I will have blue icing for the water with bubbles made of sugar balls and pink icing. The oven is set, so I open the door and place the cupcakes inside.

After the oven timer goes off, I place the hot cupcake pan on top of the stove to cool. I then frost all of them while I wait for Luca's to finish baking.

It is about five o'clock, and I finish placing the cupcakes in a plastic cupcake carrier, except for Luca's. His cake is special, and I place it in a container of its own with a note. I am hopeful this will be what I need it to be. An apology, a thank-you, to a future friendship and maybe something more. I head to the front door and step out into the warm evening with newfound hope. I place the two containers on the passenger seat and close the door. I get on the driver's side, but before I leave, I text Ryan to make sure he is still there and Luca is gone for the day. Once I get confirmation, I start my car and head to the firehouse.

I pull up to a visitor's parking spot and text Ryan that I have arrived. A few minutes later, I see him come outside. I get out and grab the cupcakes from the other side. "Okay, I hope everyone likes my cupcakes," I comment.

"I don't think you need to worry about that," he responds with a smile. "Did you want to leave whatever you have for Luca in his locker? He will be here tomorrow around noon."

"That would be amazing. I don't want the other guys to get jealous." I chuckle.

We head to the kitchen where a few of the guys are getting the rest of their dinner ready. The smell of homemade spaghetti sauce reminds me of when I was young. I would get home from school, and as soon as I opened our front door, the smell of homemade sauce would almost push me over. I smile at the memory and watch the guys zoom around the kitchen as if that is their real reason for being here. They stop and say hello when I place the container of sweet treats on the table. One asks what I brought, and when I tell him, an in-sync "mmmm" falls over the kitchen.

Ryan takes me down the hall to where their lockers are. Luca's locker has "Monts" written on the front, and Ryan swings it open for me. I put the box inside and hope for the best.

We walk back downstairs, and Ryan stops me before he walks me outside. He is a good-looking guy, blond hair, tall, with soft brown eyes. He is built just like the rest of the guys he works with: muscle-bound. I have never seen Ryan nervous, but today he seems off.

"I was hoping you could do me a favor," he starts. "I keep you in the loop, and we are good enough friends. I feel like I can ask—"

"Spit it out, darling. You do not have to convince me to do you any favors. I will happily help any way I can. Within reason."

"Would you find out if Mel is seeing anyone? I don't think she is, but I want to be sure."

"Mel is my best friend, and I know for a fact she is not seeing anybody, not even casually. I think it would do you both some good if you ask her out. I catch how she looks at you when she thinks no one is paying attention," I confirm.

"I will give her a call then. Thanks, Sun." He kisses my cheek and walks me to my car.

I pat his shoulder, telling him he and Mel could use something more interesting to do than keep an eye on Luca and me. I open my car door and slide in. Ryan closes it and smiles as I pull away.

Luca

On my way home from work, my mind is taken over by Sunny and how I am going to fix this mess. I need a shower and a scotch. I walk into my house and head down the hall to my bathroom. I take off my clothes from work and step into the shower. I smell like smoke from the fire today. The water feels amazing after the busy week I had. I wet my hair and stand under the water, hoping it will wash Sunny from my thoughts. No such luck. I need to release this feeling, so I start working myself, base to tip. Up and down, up and down. I pick up my pace as thoughts of her in the bubble bath sneak their way in. The way she felt against my body, her soft skin glistening under the dim lights of her bathroom. After thirty seconds of thinking about her, I finish all over the shower floor. I contemplate going to Hounds and picking myself up a warm body for the night. I need a break from my mind.

An hour later, I am at the bar and back to my ways. I see a girl sitting at a table to the right. Nice long legs, blond hair. She is drinking a dark beer and laughing at something her friend had said. She is nowhere near what I am looking for. I am being picky tonight. I walk up to the bar and take an empty seat in front of Char.

"Hey, darlin'." Charlotte smiles as she puts a napkin on the bar in front of me.

"Hey, Char. How are you, lovely?" I ask, leaning in for our routine cheek kiss.

"Luca, you better stop being so charming. You make a girl nervous." She blushes.

"So I've heard. Can I get a scotch?" I wink.

She grabs the good stuff she keeps under the bar. She won't take her eyes off me. Talk about making someone nervous.

"Something you want to talk about, Char?" I lean on the bar.

"Mel is here looking for you. I'm pretty sure she wants to rip your head off. She was yelling something about you staying at Sunny's a few weeks ago, taking a bubble bath with her after you got her drunk. Is that why you got everything to go that day?"

"It's not what you think. It's not what Mel thinks," I reply gruffly. I finish my glass and slide the empty glass back to Char. She quickly refills it. "Is Sunny with her?" I have a little too much hope in my voice, and Char catches on and cocks her head to the side. I shake my head before she says something smart.

"Nope. Sorry, lover boy. Another drink?" She smiles.

I am going to have to drink, and fast, if Mel is here, especially if Sun or Ryan isn't here as a buffer. I know she thinks I took advantage of Sunny, no matter what Sunny told her. It won't matter what I tell her either. She will argue that I never should have been in Sunny's tub or her bed. She is one of those women who think they know everything. It must be her red hair. I fucking hate her.

I keep drinking at a decent pace, scanning the bar and getting busier as the night goes on. Char stops in front of me every few minutes, checking to see if my glass is empty. I want to find a girl with long dark hair—preferably small, stupid, and drunk. I know I can't have Sunny even though I think I will do just about anything for her. For now, I will have to settle for someone else quenching my thirst. More like I'll be quenching her thirst. I crack myself up sometimes.

I sit at the bar for a couple of hours, watching each woman in the place. A few come over and stand too close to me while ordering their drinks. They "accidentally" bump my arm and flash a smile only they think is sexy. I am not into it tonight, but fuck it. I'll take one of them home.

I turn to my right, where a not-sexy smile awaits. When I see her, I'm surprised it took her this long to come to talk to me. Her fiery red hair flies behind her as she struts up with her hands on her hips. Her lips are pinched tightly together, and her eyes are narrowed. I am officially in her crosshairs.

Before she can open her mouth, I smile. "Hello, devil. Isn't it usually a busy night in hell? What are you doing up here?"

She gives me a look that tells me I need to stop talking. I think smoke is going to pour out of her ears. It is comical.

"You son of a bitch," she shrieks in anger. "What were you thinking, you sick fuck? She needed someone to take care of her, not try to cop some cheap feels. You just picked her up from the hospital. She just had a miscarriage, and all you care about is getting her naked," she fumes.

"First of all, I did take care of her. Very good care. Secondly, I very well could have copped as many feels as I wanted because she was so out of it, but I didn't. I didn't even look at her body, and trust me, I wanted to. When I held her, I had her by her waist. Were you there for her that night, you fucking cu—" I stop before I yell the wrong thing and get myself punched.

"Go ahead. Finish what you were going to say. Please give me a reason to hit you. Stay the hell away from her," she threatens.

Her eyes widen, and I know I need to back off this conversation with Mel now. I've never hit a woman, but things have been changing lately.

"Mel, go fuck yourself. Stop sticking your nose where it doesn't belong." I turn around and go back to my drink.

Mel turns around and takes her stiletto-wearing ass to bother a group of well-dressed men in the corner. I do not understand what Ryan sees in her. She ruined what little drive I did have to find a stupid drunk girl to take home, but it is getting late anyway. I finish one last glass of scotch, tip Char, and head home. I think I will walk tonight.

I decide to take a longer way home—up Magnolia Boulevard and through the neighborhood of Hills Manor to my neighborhood, Arden Grove. Most people have their lights out or their curtains drawn, except for one house. Sunny's house, of course. A bright glow shines where all else is dark, on top of the only hill in town, offering an uplifting metaphor for my life as it stands.

Just keep walking toward the light. You will get to where you need to be, I remind myself.

I am a couple of houses away from her lit window when I hear the music. I want to keep walking, but I make the mistake of looking. The sheer curtains trying to cover the oversized picture window do not cover anything. Light from her ceiling fan leaves little of her naked body to my imagination. Her long hair brushes her delicate waist as she sways to the rhythm of the music and drinks from a bottle of wine. Her trim legs beg my mind to wonder what they would feel like squeezing my head as she squirms with pleasure. She places the wine bottle on the floor next to her and pulls her hair up in a loose bun. Her act reveals her perfect breasts with tightened pink nipples. I am in a trance. I'm glad I didn't look at her while we were in her tub. I wouldn't have been able to stop myself, and she really would have hated me.

She takes one hand and places it between her slightly open legs and starts touching herself. I want her more than I have ever wanted anyone. I want to take all her pain away and give her what she thinks no one besides Jake can give: love and acceptance. I can feel my cock swelling as my pants tighten. My heart pounds in my chest, and my body tingles as all rationale leaves me. My hands are moist with anticipation of what she will do next. No woman has ever made me sweat like this. I need to adjust myself and walk away, but she does something to me. She always has. Watching her makes me feel devious. I miss the adrenaline rush, the excitement. I know I shouldn't be standing here acting as if she is *my* stripper, but I don't want to tear myself away.

I wonder if her door is unlocked. What would she do if I push open her door and take her right now? The only clear thought swirling in my brain is what her mouth would feel like wrapped around my girth. She would take me in like she was made for me, made to indulge my every want.

My hand finds its way down the outside of my jeans. I give myself a quick tug before I reach down my pants and adjust myself so I can walk. I stalk toward her door, keeping my eyes on her every move. I don't stop my hand from gripping my engorged devil stick. My stomach tightens, and I reach for the handle. It moves.

Why didn't she lock her door? Is she nuts?

I stand contemplating for a few minutes whether I should just go in and tell her everything, but I see one light go off. Then the music stops, and I freeze. I let go of the handle as quietly as possible and try not to move. I hold my breath as she turns the lock. Then it is dark inside. I bury the agonizing natural reaction to this situation when I realize I am being a complete drunken pervert. Rubbing my face, I walk toward the street, knowing I can't have her and it's my fault.

Sunny

A couple days after I dropped off the cupcakes, I start feeling the stress of my upcoming art show. I need to get out of the gallery. I need fresh air. Ann is in the back, getting supplies to plan out how the gallery will be set up for the best use of space. I let Ann know I am leaving for a bit and that I will be back soon.

I wonder around town for a while. I can't stop thinking about Luca. He texted me a thank-you the other day when he saw the mini cake I left for him. He told me it was amazing and that if the art gallery ever went under, I could open a bakery. I am elated my gift worked as I needed it to.

I just want him to hold me the way he did that night—all the time. I can fall for him easily. I have already started to. I have never seen this side of him. I wonder if many people have. His family, I'm sure, and the guys at the firehouse. He was so sweet and caring that night, but he's not that kind of guy.

As Luca ravages my mind, a knot forms in my stomach, but not in a bad way as I would expect. No. This is like a boy you like in school, and the only reason you go to class is because of him. *What would Jake think? Would he be mad? Why do I feel like I'm cheating on him?*

I find myself in front of Hounds. It's 3:00 p.m. But after the week I've had, I tell myself I can relax for a few minutes. As I open the door, the smell of beer and men smack me in the face, making me feel alive as if the bar has magic powers.

"Hey, Sunny," Char said, bouncing over.

"Hey, Charlotte. How's it going?" I sit down on the red seat cushion on the barstool. "Can I get a glass of Pinot?"

"Coming right up." Char grabs a glass and fills it well above the norm and puts it in front of me. "Not to be whatever," she states, "but I'm glad you weren't with Mel when she blew up on Luca. I've never seen her that angry."

My fingers run up and down the stem of the glass as I'm looking into my wine, hoping it will show me my future. "Honestly, Char, I don't know why she is so angry," I vent, rubbing my temples. "I needed him, and he was there. Nothing more and nothing less. He took care of me all weekend and took me to my doctor's appointment on Monday morning. Not once did he do anything to upset me or make me feel like something bad was about to happen. To my surprise, he made me feel safe." I pick up the glass and tip it to my lips and let the cold wine freeze the feelings that are coming up.

Char fills me in on how Luca has been acting lately. She informs me Luca has not picked up a barely legal since the night he picked up our food. She rambles on about how something has changed, and she thinks it has everything to do with me. She says that when he talks about me, his eyes widen, and his tone becomes soft. She has a sweet way of looking at the world, I think.

"Luca never had a thing for me." I gently place my empty glass on the bar and see if I can get Char to understand the relationship Luca and I have. "Did he mention," I continue, "he used to constantly put me down. And one day, I got so tired of it, I threatened to break his nose?"

A smile comes over my face at the memory. Never have I felt as empowered as I did that day. "It was during our lunch period, and I was so tired of his shit. Every day it was something else—my clothes, my hair. He said something that day that got my blood boiling, and I stood on the lunch table so I could meet his eyes, and I told him if he didn't shut up, I was going to break his nose. I don't think many people stood up to Luca. He didn't hold anything back. I, however, felt amazing after I did it. My hands shook, and he looked at me like I stabbed him in the heart. He then said, 'Come on. It's my birthday.' So I wished him a happy birthday and told him to go fuck himself. It was a proud moment for me." I smile as I replay the scene like an old movie.

Char laughs. "No, he did not tell me that. I can see why he didn't. Like I said, I think he has a thing for you. Sounds like he has for a long time."

I then proceed to tell her that I kicked him out after the second night we spent together and was rather rude about it. I also admit that he has been taking over my thoughts ever since. I share with her my apology to him after I felt so horrible for how I treated him.

"I understand. But I think how he has been since that day shows he is distraught over how things went. I know I'm just the nosy bartender, but maybe you should talk to him instead of baking him sweet treats," she pushes.

"Charlotte, you are more than a bartender. More like the town shrink," I joke. "And I know you are right. I do need to talk to him and maybe trust him, eventually."

Char's eyes widen, and she leans over the bar and whispers, "Speak of the devil. Luca just walked in."

I swallow the last bit of wine and pay Char. "That's my cue. Thanks, Char. See you later."

I get up and turn to leave when I suddenly find myself facing Luca's chest. "Hey, sorry. How are you?" I smile, noticing a smug smirk on his face. He makes me nervous, and for some reason, that turns me on more than I want it to. I can feel my body react to him and become wet with desire.

Does he know what he does to me? I try to look comfortable, but he can see right through my lies.

"I ate your apology," he starts. "It was delicious and hit the spot. I hope you know I am forgiving you strictly because of the icing—a bubble bath cake. You are thoughtful, aren't you?"

He holds me gently by my upper arm, close so I can't just run by unscathed. I am so nervous, my throat tightens, and I am barely able to tell him I am glad he enjoyed it.

"How could I not like it?" he asks. "It reminds me of that night."

As much as I don't want to admit it, that night is all I dream about.

He tries to get me to stay and have a drink with him, but I tell him I can't. It is a massive lie. Ann knows I am taking a long lunch today. I am still terrified of him—well, my feelings for him. I stumble over my words, and he lets my arm go, looking like a lost puppy.

I let him know I will be at the gallery every day this week if he wants to stop by, feeling like I will be more comfortable in my own space.

I turn and walk out as fast as I can. When I get outside, the cool breeze of the day calms my nerves. I take a few deep breaths, inhaling as deeply as my lungs will allow.

What in the hell? Have a drink with him? No, we aren't there yet.

I take my phone out of the bag that is strung across my chest and call Mel. She will talk sense into me; she always does. I start walking back to the gallery when she picks up. She sounds out of breath. She fills me in on how she has decided to take up running. Ryan told her how much he enjoys it, and she decided to go for it.

I have a feeling Ryan did that on purpose, and it is getting the desired effect. I have a way in to ask her if she is running with Ryan. I want to pry some gossip out of her. I need to live vicariously through her, at least until I can focus on a life of dating.

"Did he say something?" she inquires.

"Maybe. What's it worth to ya?" I tease.

"Please, Sun. Tell me. He is so damn hot. I was hoping he and I can start running together."

"I say go for it. I have complete confidence he wants to take you out. Please do something fun then tell me all about it."

"Why don't we double-date? I'm sure I can find you a date," she says, trying to entice me.

"Mel, I do not need you to find me a date. Not to mention, I am too busy with the show and all. I have to stay focused."

"Fine. All work and no play. Just don't go falling for Luca. Ryan told me about the cake. You are one of the sweetest people I know, but does he deserve that? You are such a thoughtful person, and he's…well, him."

I tell her I am not falling for Luca. The cake was just a peace offering. She bites back with the fact that I made him a special one instead of a normal one, like the others with a note. I clarify that it is unacceptable for me to not thank him and that I had to apologize to him after everything that had transpired.

I get to the gallery and pull the door open to find Ann sitting on the floor. She looks up at me through black-framed glasses and wisps of light brown hair. Her expression is that of accomplishment. She jabbers about how she has figured out the best way to set up the show for a maximum number of pieces, sculptures, and paintings alike. She has it drawn up on a large board in front of her.

I have to commend her; she is good. Ann also informs me a few writers have reached out for information on the upcoming festivities. I am more than pleased, and I feel the weight on my shoulders lessen.

Luca

Disappointed that Sunny lied and said she couldn't stay, I take a seat at the bar and ask Char to pour me a scotch. Firmly planted on the barstool, I think only of how I want to go after Sunny. Holding her for those two minutes before she walked out made me realize some drunk whore that looks like her just won't do.

Char questions the expression on my face, saying I look like a predator scoping out my prey. I act like I have no clue what she is talking about, knowing full well what I must look like. She rolls her eyes and sighs as though she is not in the mood for my games today. I shoot her a wide smile and she relaxes.

I signal for her to lean in so I can tell her my dirty secret. "So after I left here the other night, I took a different way home. I walked by her house, and her lights were on. Naturally, I stopped to look, and she was dancing naked in the window, drinking from a wine bottle. I cannot get that image out of my mind. Not that I want to. Do not say a word to anyone."

I can feel my smirk turn into a lustful smile.

"You creep! Did she see you?" Char's mouth is wide open, and her eyes look like they are going to pop out of her head.

"Nope. I know it sounds bad, but I just watched her. I couldn't take my eyes off her," I admit, leaving out the part where I turned her door handle. "The day after, Ryan calls and says he needs me to come to work. I get there and open my locker. There is a mini cake that is blue with pink icing bubbles on the top. A bubble bath. There was also a note that went with it. She wrote that it was a peace offering. She dropped it off earlier that day."

"Uh-huh. So are you going to do anything about this peace offering?"

"Char, she doesn't trust me. She has good reason, but I don't think they should be valid anymore. People can change, you know."

"I know," Char agrees. "You certainly did a number on her, huh?"

"I did." I hang my head like a child who just got caught stealing candy. "I need to talk to her when she is alone. I might stop by her gallery on Wednesday, take her up on her offer."

"What offer?" Char pries.

"She told me she couldn't stay for a drink today but that she will be at the gallery all week. I think I will do something about her peace offering."

My head fills with nasty thoughts of what Wednesday could look like. I finish my drink and head home.

*****

Wednesday is finally here, and the last few days at the firehouse have been busy. There was a massive fire that broke out in the next town, and they called us to help them out. When we got there, another fire company had shown up as well. I am looking forward to some time alone with Sunny, especially since I am not seeing her because something is wrong.

I pull up to the gallery at eight thirty and park on the street behind Sunny's car. The familiar chime sounds as I step through the door. Sunny comes out from the back with a smile on her face. This time, it doesn't fade. I can see her entire body tense when she sees me. I pull the wine and scotch from the paper bag, telling her it was time we got to know each other better. I place the alcohol on the counter to my right and wait for her to say something. She looks terrified. This may take a few minutes.

Then her body relaxes. "Trying to get me drunk again," she jokes. She grabs two glasses from under the counter and cracks open the bottle of scotch and pours the first round. The stools are comfortable with thick black cushions. To answer her question honestly, yes, I am—but only so she can relax.

I smile, remembering the night she danced in the window. How she looked like she didn't have a care in the world reminded me of the old Sunny bouncing down the halls of our high school. I know I can't remain on that thought too long or I will not make her feel safe. That is the most important thing right now.

I realize she is pouring herself a scotch as well, and I look at her, confused. She confesses that wine won't do it tonight. She wants to talk but admits I make her nervous. Fair enough. We raise our glasses to building a better relationship.

We have a few drinks before we get into a "getting to know you" conversation. The short black skirt and the form-fitting black button-down top she is wearing make it hard for me to concentrate on what I want to say to her. I start telling her about how, after high school, my parents shipped me off to the military. I had served four years when I met Sarah. I retired, moved home, and became a firefighter.

She recalls when she met Jake a few months after graduation. She smiles, remembering how they were taken by each other immediately when they were introduced during an art retreat. She tells me about the gallery and how long it took to renovate the place. She proudly tells me about the show she had not long ago, raising money for local artists, and her adult carnival show that is coming up. I can't help how I feel about her, and I am going to tell her as soon as I clear my conscience.

I put my glass on the counter and slide it over to Sunny for a refill. She happily obliges my unspoken request. I need to tell her the truth about that night and what started everything. I ask her to come out from the other side of the counter and sit next to me. I have never been as nervous to tell someone something as I am at this moment. I don't want what I have to say to ruin the progress we have made tonight.

She walks out from behind the counter with uncertainty. It's cute and it turns me on. She stands next to me, and I pull the black stool out for her. She sits down and crosses her legs, placing one arm on the counter, looking at me with intensity. My body reacts with a wave of lust that floods my thoughts. I struggle to keep myself from touching her before I tell her, knowing that if I start, I won't stop.

"I have to come clean about something," I start. "It is my fault we are in this situation." Her eyes grow sad, and confusion covers her face as I continue, "I wanted to apologize at the reunion. That's why I came over to you. When Sarah and I got home, we got into it badly, worse than ever before. She accused me of trying to pick you up in front of her. I tried to explain, but she wanted no part of it. I am not a great guy, you know that I know that, but I was trying to make up for the shitty things I did. I had been trying to be a better husband to her, but it wasn't enough. I truly am sorry. I never meant for any of this to happen."

She sits for a minute, her expression blank. Her mouth curls into a smile, and now I'm confused.

"She thought you were hitting on me?" She laughs. "I'm sorry. I don't mean to laugh, but really?"

"Is that so outlandish to you?" I challenge.

"Yes, it is," she barks, shattering me like I am made of glass. "Not to mention, if the accident is your fault, and that is your reasoning why, then it is my fault too. I was craving cookie dough ice cream when we got home. Jake was the kind of guy who would and did drop everything to make me happy. It's part of why I loved him. He treated me like his queen. He grabbed his keys, kissed me, and was out the door before I could talk him out of going. So you see, if it is your fault, then it is my fault too. I know you think I'm weird, but I believe that things happen for a reason. Maybe it is just my way of coping with things. I have noticed, if you are patient, the reason shows itself eventually."

She takes my hand in hers. For once, it is not trembling. She turns it so that the back of my hand is in her right palm. She starts to trace circles in my hand with her left index finger. I don't understand why, but I can't help but smile.

She explains that she would go into his office, usually late at night, and sit across from him at his desk. She'd say, "Mr. Thompson, may I see your hand?" Then he would reply, "Mrs. Thompson, you have perfect timing." Sunny would turn his hand so the back of it was in her palm. Then she would instruct him to close his eyes while using her other hand to trace circles in his palm. It was at that moment, every time, the corners of his lips would curl and his body visibly relaxed. Then she would tell him a story that involved two lovers. He ended this ritual by kissing her hand and telling her he wouldn't know how to get through his days without her.

Her touch, when she's not sobbing in my chest, is healing. I can feel the warmth from her traveling through my entire body. I take a deep breath and put my other hand on top of hers. I have something else to tell her. I know I am probably jumping the gun, but I'll deal with the consequences.

"I have another confession if you want to hear it," I say.

"It depends. I don't know if I've had enough to drink." She giggles as she quickly finishes her scotch then pours another. "Okay, shoot."

"I was walking home from the bar a few nights ago"—I lock her gaze, not allowing her to look away from me—"when I happened on your house. It had been around two a.m. and, well, you should get curtains that cover your windows."

Sunny

I let go of his hand and jump out of my seat. I can feel the heat pooling in my cheeks. My body feels as though I have been lit on fire. I can't feel my legs but am all too aware of what's going on between them. I demand to know how long he was standing there and what he saw. I don't know what I hope to accomplish with this knowledge, but I ask anyway.

Luca's eyes darken, and his smile is replaced by what I can only describe as devious intentions. He stands up and is only a few inches away from me. "Long enough." He towers over me, and I can tell he enjoys keeping me on edge.

He starts to slowly stalk toward me. I can't look away from him, his eyes piercing mine. I am afraid if I look away, it will give him enough time to do whatever it is he plans on doing. I don't know if I would stop him. The closer he gets, the hotter my body burns. I can feel a lump in my throat. My breathing becomes labored as I try to back away slowly, but I soon realize it is turning him on even more. He adjusts himself as he gets closer, making it clear what he wants. He still terrifies me. He looks like a madman with a new toy to play with.

"Are you going to answer me?" I manage to squeeze out as my back hits a wall. *Nowhere to go now.*

Luca pins me between himself and the wall, not being able to restrain himself from rubbing his cock against my stomach. He puts his forefinger under my chin and tilts my head back, forcing me to look at him. The heat being released from his body and the way his rough hands feel on my skin make me forget everything he has ever said to me, everything that has happened.

He brushes my hair behind my shoulders and delicately unbuttons my blouse. My nipples tighten from his touch. It is getting harder to breathe, and I am frozen. He slides my blouse off and stands back, staring at me like an animal before it goes in for the kill. He runs his hands down the front of my chest, pinching my nipples between his fingers. I can't stop trembling, and he loves every second of it. I place my hands against his chest. His skin is hot with a craving I am afraid I can't satisfy. Will this be something else for him to use against me? I hate my thoughts going there, but I can't help it.

As if he can read my mind, he leans close and kisses my body softly, starting a fire in me that never should have been there. I can feel his hands grip my waist, pulling me even closer to him as he kisses his way to my neck. Feeling as though we can't get any closer, he leans more of his weight against me, making sure I can't get away.

"What are you doing?" I ask, not wanting this to stop.

"What I should have done a long time ago," he answers, not skipping a kiss.

"What's that?" I breathlessly whisper.

He swallows my mouth in a deep kiss that makes the world disappear. I hear the zipper of his pants come down, and he pulls his cock out. He grabs my shaking hand and guides me to feel how much he wants me. Luca pushes himself farther against me as I give his cock a light tug.

He lightly kisses my neck as I take my free hand and claw at his back. Our breathing is heavy, drowning out any background noise. He pulls my skirt up and uses his knee to spread my legs. I can't help but let him feel how turned on I am as he reaches between my legs and slides two fingers inside of me. My breath catches in my throat as I try not to make too much noise. Ann is upstairs.

My hands pull at his hair because his touch is overwhelming. As he slides his fingers out of me at a tormenting pace, he leans in and whispers "turn around" while nibbling at my ear. I do what he quietly commands. I will do anything he asks. I refuse to deny him any longer. It's about time he made me feel good.

He grips himself and lifts the back of my skirt. "Bend over for me, beautiful," he demands. As soon as I do, he starts rubbing his thickness on my dripping wet entrance. He finds my clit and rubs himself against it, making my knees weak. I want to get lost in him. *I never want this to end.*

"Maybe we should go in the back," I suggest breathlessly.

We stumble to the back studio, never taking our mouths away from each other, slamming the door behind us. He tears himself from my lips and drops to his knees. Grabbing my skirt from the top, he rips it down to the floor. He lifts my right leg and places it on his shoulder. I feel his tongue start to taste me, and I swear my legs will give out. My hands grip his hair tightly as his right arm rests on my lower back, keeping me steady. Just when he is about to push me over the edge, he stops and warns me he's not done playing with me yet.

Standing up, he wraps his thick arms around me and tosses me onto the bed in the corner, which I have in case I get too tired to drive home when I am here late. I land on my back and prop myself up on my elbows so I can watch him undress. His shirt first, then pants, then boxers—I can't take my eyes off him. *Nobody should be that good-looking.*

He struts over to me, and with the low rumble of his voice, he says, "Spread your legs, my good girl."

I open my legs, and he gets down and continues to taste me. With his head between my legs and his hands under me, I can't help but tense around his head. He stops and looks up at me with the most sinister smile I have ever seen. He then buries his head back where it was.

I have never felt like this in my life. I don't know if it is because I can finally stop criticizing myself since Luca finally gave me validation that I am not the things he said. Maybe it's because I haven't been touched in months, or it's a combination of the two. I push the questions out of my head and decide to enjoy him. Even if it's only once.

Luca

When Sunny tenses around my head, I stop so I can take in the sight of her from this angle. I haven't stopped imagining this moment since I saw her in the window. I am never this generous to a woman, not even Sarah. Sunny is dripping wet and begging me to fuck her, but I'm not done playing with her yet. I lick my way up her body, tasting every inch of her, and damn is she tasty. I stop at her nipples, lowering my head, sucking on one and then the other. I end my journey at her lips and then invade her mouth with my tongue. I put two fingers inside of her, not giving her anywhere to go. She is what I wanted all along.

"How bad do you want me, Sunny?"

"More than you know. I haven't felt like this in a long time."

"Me either." I bury my head in her chest. "Do you like it rough?" I ask while I continue to tease her.

"Do you like it when I'm in pain?" A devilish smile creeps across her face as she bites her lip and pulls me closer.

"Only if I'm the one controlling it," I confess.

"Why does that turn me on?" She is trying to catch her breath but losing the battle.

"Because you secretly want me to take advantage of you. Is that why you danced in your window? I wanted to come in and take you then. Maybe I should have. There was nothing you could have done, and I think you like that." I move so my throbbing girth is at her chin. "Open your mouth, my good girl."

Sunny smiles, knowing I am right. She does as she is told.

I know she likes being overpowered and feeling out of control. I enjoy her talented mouth for a minute until I feel myself needing to be inside her warmth. "Sunny, I can't wait any longer," I whisper as I pull myself from her mouth. I spread her legs farther apart and thrust myself deep inside her tight pussy. Sunny moans as she grabs my hair. My hand covers her mouth, not wanting her to wake Ann up. It's late.

We complement each other well. I tell her what to do, and she listens. She will let me do things—things I can't talk the twentysomethings into doing. I gently pull out of her and demand she get on all fours. She does as she is told without question, and that is dangerous for her.

She's bent over, and I place a pillow under her hips to tilt her the way I want her. I grab a fistful of her hair and decide to explore her back door. I take some of her wetness from where I had just been and trace my fingers around my new target. I instruct her to take a deep breath and relax. I gently work one finger inside her, then a second. I play with her, making sure not to hurt her. Once I am sure she is not in pain, I thrust my cock inside her. I feel her body tense uncontrollably, and she quivers around my cock. She is moaning, and I am finding it difficult to last much longer. I'd like to push her boundaries more, but I don't want her to get scared. Not just yet anyway. Feeling Sunny under me is how things should have been all along.

I pull out of her and come all over the plump ass bent over in front of me. We flop over on the bed, trying to catch our breath. I take her by the waist and pull her close to me, wrapping my arms around her. Is this what it was supposed to be like all along? I like the thought of being with her and her alone.

"Luca?" she whispers.

"Yeah?" I turn to her as she yawns, still trying to regain complete use of her lungs.

"Do you want to come over to my house, and I'll make us breakfast?"

"How about I call over to the diner and we can pick breakfast up on the way back to your house?"

She looks pleased and tells me what she wants. She gets up to get dressed, but I lie there, taking in the beautiful sight of her.

Sunny

After we get back to my place, I go straight to the spacious kitchen and unpack the unbelievable amount of food he ordered. After we eat, I ask him to come upstairs and lie with me for a while. He happily agrees but suggests we get a shower before falling asleep. I do not argue. That sounds like exactly what we need.

By the time we make it to my bedroom, we are exhausted, feeling drunk on endorphins but weighed down by our hearty breakfast. It has been a long and interesting twenty-four hours. This time, I grab his hand and lead the way to the shower. I let my clothes fall to the bathroom floor and step into the shower stall. Looking over my shoulder, I ask, "You are coming?"

"Yes, ma'am," Luca confirms, taking his clothes off. As he comes up behind me, he places his hands on my hips and says, "Is it still so wrong that I hit on you? It felt a little more than right to me."

"I never knew you felt like that. You were such a dick." I giggle. "I can't deny it feels right. The only thing that has in the past few months."

More than anything ever has, if I'm being honest. But I'm not telling him that. I turn to him and take the soap from the dish mounted to the wall behind him. I soap up my washcloth and seductively go about washing myself, pushing him away each time he reaches for me. Rinsing off under the water, I close my eyes and feel him behind me with his bearlike grip around my body.

"Not yet," I say, pushing my ass against him. I feel him getting aroused again. He's about to be very satisfied.

He lets go and takes a step back. Turning around, I push him farther back and then guide him to stand under the showerhead. I take my time washing every inch of him, teasing him the entire time. I don't let him touch me or himself. I can see the darkness take over his eyes as he grows more and more needful. I drop to the tiled floor and take him in my mouth, relaxing my throat so I can take every inch of him in. He grabs the back of my head and has a tight hold on my hair. I cup his balls, working my magic. He squeezes my shoulder with his free hand and loses control of himself. After I stand up, he shuts the water off and kisses my lips softly.

I take two towels from the cabinet under the vanity and throw him one. We dry off, and I drop my towel on the floor as I open the bathroom door and escort him to my bed. The sun is bright, so I close the blinds and the room-darkening curtains. I turn and see he left his towel somewhere as well. He lifts the sheets and signals for me to get in. Like before, I don't argue, and he slides in after me. I lie on my side, and he makes himself *my* blanket, wrapping me in his strong embrace. He kisses the back of my head and tells me to get some rest. He is off the next few days and is planning on helping Ann and me set up for the upcoming show. He also tells me, whatever I need to be done for the show, he will take care of it. I just need to let him know.

I wonder if he ever treated anyone like this before. He has never been known to be sweet or romantic, but he has been nothing but just that since the accident. He never stopped trying to make sure I was doing well—as well as I could be. Ryan let it slip the other day that he had been keeping Luca informed of how I was doing. That is the main reason I am not going crazy, wondering if he means what he says.

I put one arm under my pillow, and the other is resting on Luca's arm that wraps around me, keeping me close. We fall asleep in each other's comfort once again.

Sunny

The beautiful summer sky is being taken over by the comfort of dusk. The carnival show has been underway for about an hour, but I still have yet to see Luca. At this point, the show is just as much his as it is mine. He has worked hard to help me get everything ready for the show, from displaying the paintings and sculptures to replacing the light fixtures. All this and working full-time have been exhausting for him. I'll reward him later. I pour a glass of champagne for myself and figure it's time to make my first round.

I step out from behind the new bar that has taken the place of the temporary counter. Luca made the bar his project. He said that if you have an upscale gallery that serves, you need an upscale bar to go with it. So far tonight, it has come in handy, especially with the amount of alcohol being served. I hired a catering company complete with a bartender on Char's recommendation.

I weave my way through the maze of temporary walls lined with sculptures of nude women with oversized breasts and protruding pubic bones. The sculptures of the men also focus on emphasized genitalia, some gigantic and some looking inadequate. My favorite sculpture so far is one of a giant with a modest penis and a woman with voluptuous breasts on her knees in front of him. Most of the sculptures are of individuals, but the paintings have a life all their own. From naked bearded ladies to unmistakable visions of blatant sexuality.

The place is packed to capacity with the women wearing gowns accentuating their bodies, breasts pushed up to their chins, and slits of the dresses going to their hips. The men wear tuxedos and top hats, lustfully clinging to the women who will surely act as the dutiful concubines later tonight.

Luca helped me pick out my dress because I couldn't decide which one to buy. It is a black skintight dress with long sleeves and a deep V-neck that goes to my waist. It is backless, and the bottom skirt has a single string of red crystals on each side, keeping the front and back held in place. I can feel the pain in my feet creeping in because tonight, I decided to wear stilettos, which I normally don't do. My hair is in a French twist, and my makeup is bold with my fake eyelashes reaching my brows. I am starting to worry. Luca got off work two hours ago.

As I round the last corner of the sculptures, I see Mel. She is wearing a shimmering green dress that makes her cascading red hair look more fiery than usual. Her porcelain skin is radiating with happiness, and when I look to her right, I can see why. Ryan is beside her with his hand resting on her low back, his cheeks red with excitement. They are talking to another couple, but their backs are to me so I can't tell who it is. As I make my way over to them, my ears are filled with the sounds of drunken laughter and erotic banter.

Mel and Ryan excitedly greet me with hugs, kisses, and compliments. I turn to thank the couple behind me for coming and realize it is Char and Jimmy. More hugs, kisses, and compliments on the show. Still having a pit of worry in my stomach, I ask them if anyone has seen or heard from Luca. As they all shake their heads, I can feel Luca's muscular arms wrapping around my waist from behind, forcing my body against his. He says hello to everyone before he drops his voice and puts his lips to my ear, complimenting me on how amazing the gallery looks and that I pulled it off without a hitch. My arms still resting on his, he sweetly kisses my cheek. It makes me smile, but I turn my head so I can look into his soft eyes and remind him that if it wasn't for him and Ann, none of this would have happened.

Luca lets go of my waist and takes my small hand in his, excusing us from the group. He leads me down another row of temporary walls where we run into Ann. She is talking with some of the reporters that came out to see what we do here. I have never seen her so full of life. Her hair and makeup are astonishing, and her purple gown makes her look like a young seductress. We exchange proud looks for our accomplishment this evening.

Luca and I reach the closed door that leads to my studio. He opens the door, shuffling me inside. He closes and locks the door behind him. I turn so I can get a good look at the handsome man who helped me pull this event off. He doesn't disappoint. His hair is slicked back under his top hat, which he tosses on the chair against the wall. He grabs my hands and takes a step back so he can study the dress he picked out. He seems satisfied with his choice.

"You look delicious in that dress. Now be my good girl and take it off," he demands.

I do as he instructs. I slide the dress off my body and onto the floor. I wasn't able to wear a bra or panties tonight, so there isn't much to take off. I step out of it so he can see me in nothing but my black stilettos. He licks his lips while he takes off his jacket and dress shirt. He then lays them on the chair where his top hat rests. He kicks off his polished black shoes and stalks toward me. Standing only a few inches from me, I can feel his hunger.

I tug at the top of his pants, bringing him close enough that his skin scorches mine. I unbuckle his belt and take my time unzipping his pants while his eyes burn into my soul. I can feel him getting aroused, and as I finish pulling his pants and boxers off, his cock just about jumps out of his pants as if it were being asphyxiated.

Before he can get his hands on me, I drop to my knees and take him into my mouth. A throaty groan escapes him as I suck on him like my life depended it. I suckle his tip while I keep his balls occupied, sliding my mouth up and down his shaft. He squeezes my shoulder, trying not to make a sound.

Luca

Her lips feel like heaven as she sucks on my tip, using her hands to make the pleasure more intense. A carnality I refuse to fight is rising with every twist of her tongue. My cock aches with a vengeance as I remove myself from the heat of her mouth. She looks up at me, her lips glistening from her fun.

I roughly yank her to her feet and turn her around so her back is to my chest. I use my strength to force her to the desk in the corner—not that I need to force her to do anything. I tell her to place her hands on top of the desk. Doing as she is told, I let my fingers find her hot center. She is dripping with a need I will more than satisfy. I place one hand over Sunny's mouth. My good girl can be loud, and people might hear her.

"Spread your legs and bend over, my good girl," I instruct her.

I slide into her softness, and her muscles immediately clench around my girth. I am gentle at first, but I have a surprise for her. Opening the drawer to my right, I pull out an anal toy and some lube. I hid them before I left the other night. I want to push her boundaries tonight. Keeping a soft rhythm, I lube the toys and rub some on her tight ring. As I do, I feel her body tense with anticipation of what I will do to her next.

My thrusts become slower and deeper as I suggest she take a deep breath and relax. Placing the toy in slowly, I slide it in and out of her wetness. Her body grips mine with an unexpected force. I can feel her moaning, but my hand still covers her mouth, not letting a sound slip from her bright red lips. I tighten my seal over her mouth and take her as hard as I can. Before I finish inside her, I pull out and spill onto her round ass. I grab a nearby towel and clean her off. I take my hand from her mouth, and I can only hear her trying to catch her breath.

She reaches around to her backside, wanting to take out the toy I had placed there. I snatch her arm before she can pull it out. She looks back at me, her eyes wide while I put more pressure on the toy between her cheeks.

"I want you to be my good girl again and leave this in for the rest of the night. I promise I will take it out before we go to bed," I explain.

Sunny straightens up and turns to face me. Her eyes are heavy with satisfaction, and she is looking at me like she wants more. I can't help the smirk that forms across my face. She bites her bottom lip and pushes me aside so she can get dressed. I follow her, unable to tear my eyes away from her glowing skin. After we get dressed, I unlock the door and escort her back to her show.

More people have crowded into the gallery since we snuck away. For the first time in a long while, I am truly happy. Sunny keeps me on my toes, always wanting to try new things and dragging me all over the place. I am desperate to keep her close. I spent my entire life being what everyone else wanted me to be. Sunny makes me feel free. She creates a space for me to explore life with no judgment and no insane expectations, just unconditional acceptance. The nice part is that she is by my side, supporting whatever I want to do.

A heavy hand pats my back, taking me from my thoughts of my good girl. I turn my head to find Ryan and his date standing behind us. Even though Mel makes me want to commit murder, I will admit that she looks gorgeous tonight, and it looks like Ryan is happy. They say they are going to call it a night, both looking more tired than I've ever seen them. I check my watch and see it is much later than I realized.

The show is starting to wind down, and people are making their final purchases. From the looks of things, it seems as though every piece has a Sold sign hanging from it. Sunny makes her last rounds of the night, helping the out-of-towners make a final decision on a piece that best suits them.

*****

As I finally pull up to Sunny's house, fatigue hits me like a ton of bricks. We trudge to the front door. Sunny's heels are dangling from her fingertips. She fishes her keys from her purse and fumbles to unlock the door. I follow behind her, unable to keep myself from cupping her ass as we climb the never-ending stairs. I flip the switch on the wall, and the hallway is illuminated by a soft light on the ceiling.

Dropping her shoes and bag on the floor, she turns the bedroom light on. She pulls the pins from her hair as she meanders to the bathroom a few feet away. She peeks at me over her shoulder and flashes a tantalizing grin my way. I can't help the devil fighting his way out as I stride to catch up to her. I stop her from undressing herself and taking my fun away. I put my hand on her chest and back her against the wall. The look she is giving me drives my need for her even further.

Her skin is searing with arousal that, in turn, rekindles my need to be inside her. I peel her dress from her curvy body. My cock hardens, needing her touch. As if she is reading my thoughts, she unbuckles my belt. We stare into each other's eyes as her dress falls to the floor. She steps out of it and pushes my arms to my sides.

She proceeds to slide my jacket off as she moves to unbutton my shirt. Taking her time, she unzips my pants and pushes them to the floor, making a point to touch everything except my rock-hard cock. Her games have me wanting to dominate her as she slips under my arm and struts to the shower. She bends over to turn the water on, and I catch a glimpse of the metal toy still lodged inside her.

Sunny

Before I can stand up straight, Luca is behind me. My heart pounds harder every time he touches me. His arm is around me as his other hand fondles the toy that he placed inside me earlier. I had a hard time keeping myself under control after he took me in the middle of the show. I need him now. His touch is dominating and forceful. He makes me feel like I am the only one he wants.

Luca asks if I want him to take the plug out. Being as tired as I am, I say yes. As he removes the plug bit by bit, I am reminded why I don't play with these toys often. I can feel my body trying to relax so he doesn't hurt me. My knees buckle at the sting of the toy as he finishes taking it out. Luca tightens his grip around me as the nausea sets in.

Placing the metal toy on the ledge, he grabs the soap from the dish. His large hands cover every inch of my body as he washes most traces down the drain. I am exhausted from the night. I lean against him, unable to stand on my own. He steadies me with one arm. His touch is soft and sweet. When he finishes, he kisses my forehead and tells me to dry off and wash my face while he finishes up.

Doing as I am told, I get out and wrap my tired body in the warmth of my towel. I peel the fake lashes from my eyelids and let them fall into the trash can to the left of the vanity. I scrub the makeup off my face, feeling like I have been reborn. I hear the water from the shower turn off, and before I know it, Luca is behind, rubbing his erection against me. Smiling, I look at his reflection in the mirror in front of us.

"Let's get in bed, my good girl," he whispers, kissing the back of my neck.

Being as tired as I am, I am surprised my body reacts to him telling me we need to go to bed. I can feel my center becoming hot and moist with anticipation of his touch. I escort him to the bed and lie down. He then takes his place next to me. I roll onto my side so I can get lost in his eyes. They are my favorite place to get lost in. He runs his rough hands through my hair as my hand finds its way to his needy member.

"My good girl," he starts. "I know you are tired. We don't have to do this right now."

"I want to. I want to make you happy," I respond.

"What makes you think I'm not happy?" he questions. His eyes dim, and his brow furrows.

I try to explain how afraid I am of losing another person I care about, whatever the reason. My cheeks become hot, and tears form in my eyes. His expression relaxes, and the corners of his mouth curl. He points out that this is the first time I admitted I cared for him. To my surprise, I care for him more than I ever expected. My feelings for him are growing stronger every day.

He rolls me onto my back and climbs on top of me, his weight making me feel safe. His lips are sweet when he kisses me while he pushes my legs apart, causing a strong need that invades every cell of my body. I don't understand how this happened, and I can't believe I am questioning it. We both deserve to be happy after everything Luca and I have been through.

He instructs me to lie back and tells me he will take care of me this time around. He presses his tip into my swollen entrance. My legs start to shake, and my nipples tighten at his touch. Inch by inch, he pushes himself inside me, being careful not to push too hard. He knows my body can't handle it right now.

He feels me tremble underneath him and leans down to pepper my lips with his sweet kisses. He is gentle with a steady rhythm as we enjoy the feel of him inside me one last time before we crumble onto the bed and fall asleep.

*****

The sun is blinding as it shines through the bedroom window, waking me. My phone says it is three o'clock in the afternoon, and my stomach growls with hunger. I turn to Luca still fast asleep beside me. He looks peaceful. It is a look I am not used to seeing on him. I smile, knowing he will spend the rest of the day with me before he has to go back to work tomorrow.

I slide out from his grip on me, careful not to wake him. I tiptoe to the bathroom and throw on my blue silk robe. I creep past the bed then hurry downstairs so I can make breakfast before he gets up for the day. I get to the kitchen and open the refrigerator only to see I have nothing to make. I need to get to the grocery store, especially if Luca will be here more. I love to cook, and I love it even more when I am feeding someone I love.

Whoa, love him? Do I? Can I?

I run back upstairs to find my cell phone so I can order breakfast from Maria's Diner. I am as quiet as possible, and Luca doesn't move a muscle. Once I have my phone, I head back downstairs and call for delivery. I order two bacon-and-egg combo meals, pancakes, French toast, and bagels. I don't know what he will be in the mood for, so I also order a Reuben, remembering it is his favorite sandwich. I can't believe what has developed between us, but I am happy that whatever it is, it is there.

A half hour later, there is a quiet knock at the door. I open the door to see Jaime, a young sculptor from the show last night, holding our breakfast. We chat for a few minutes about how well the show did, and Jaime informs me that if his work keeps selling the way it does, he will be able to move to the city, where he says he can shine. I reassure him that he shines already. He gives me a shy smile and thanks me for displaying his sculptures. A minute later, Jaime gets in his car, which is parked in front of the street.

When I shut the door, I see a large figure standing behind it. My stomach drops to the floor, and my heart starts racing.

"Got you." Luca laughs. I didn't hear him get up or come downstairs.

He grabs the plastic bags out of my hands and heads to the kitchen. I follow behind him, not being able to hide the smile he puts on my face.

Luca puts the bags on the counter and tells me to have a seat at the island. He starts unloading everything and bringing it to me. He goes through the cabinets and gets two plates and two coffee mugs. He pours us each coffee, which I made before our food was delivered. Luca places my mug in front of me and kisses the top of my head. When he brings the rest of the food over, he jokes about how much food I ordered.

"This looks amazing," Luca says.

"I wasn't sure what you would be in the mood for, so I ordered all kinds of food," I explain.

He grins and thanks me. We sit quietly and stuff our mouths with sweet French toast and work our way through each dish. I am glad I got all this food; we are both hungrier than we thought.

"Last night was fantastic. We ended up selling almost every piece," I excitedly tell him.

"You did a great job last night. Jake would be proud of you, gorgeous."

"I think Sarah would be pretty proud of you too. You haven't left my side in months unless it is to go to work. You built a bar for the gallery, and you got everything set up. I bet she is smiling down on you as we speak."

"I don't think she was ever proud of me," he replies.

"Hey, she would be now." I place my hands on top of his, which are resting on the island top. "Luca, you have changed. You are not that guy who picks up barely legal women. You are not that guy who doesn't care about anything. You are, sure as hell, not the same person you were three months ago."

I try to get him to understand. Time has flown by these last few months, and I am pretty sure it is because Luca and I are happy. We support each other when the weight of what happened to us crushes us to pieces. We check in with each other when we are not together. I didn't know Luca cared about anything. The past few months have opened my eyes as to what kind of man he is. Given the chance, he has proven that he is a good man.

"Thank you, gorgeous," he says, taking my hand in his and putting it to his lips. He kisses my knuckles before getting up to take care of our breakfast mess.

I get up and stand behind him then wrap my arms around the back of him. I feel Luca's body relax. He turns around and wraps his arms around me so tight, I can feel the air being pushed from my lungs. I whisper that I am going to get a shower, and he should join me. He says he will as soon as he is done in the kitchen. He pats my backside and turns back to what he was doing.

I get upstairs and let my robe fall to the floor. Then I turn the water on for the shower. After I am in and washing my hair, I feel his warm skin against mine while the water rushes over us. He pushes my arms down to my sides and proceeds to wash my hair. When he is finished washing me, I take the soap from his hand and do the same for him.

He gets out and grabs us both a towel. When I step out, he is waiting with the towel open so he can wrap me up. We get dressed and decide to watch movies in bed for the rest of the day. Luca has to work at the firehouse tomorrow, so I won't see him for two days.

Luca

Sunny and I have spent almost every day together since a month before her art show. If I had it my way, we would be engaged by now, but I don't know if she is ready for that. The day after her show, we talked about moving in together. That was a month ago, and we still haven't decided if we are going to sell both of our houses and buy a new one or if we are going to sell one and move into the other. I feel like we live together already. I stay at her house most nights.

I wake up next to my good girl on Saturday morning, and I slide out of bed so I don't wake her. I head to the bathroom and get changed for work. When I come out, Sunny is awake, her eyes heavy with sleep. I walk over to the bed and sit next to where she lies. Her smile every morning is all the sunshine I need in my life right now. I push her hair from her forehead and lean down so I can kiss her before I go. She grabs my hand and won't let go.

"What's wrong, my good girl?" I question.

Her smile fades, and tears fill her eyes. She pushes herself up so she is sitting and throws her arms around me and holds on tight. She whispers she had a bad dream. I hug her and ask her to tell me what happened that got her so upset. She goes on to tell me that in her dream, I died in a fire trying to rescue someone. I can't help but smile, making my heart burn for her. If she is worried about me, I am taking that as a good sign.

I squeeze her as hard as I can without suffocating her. I tell her she has nothing to worry about, especially now that I know I have someone wonderful to come home to. She is trying to stop crying but can't. She makes me feel loved and cared for even if she doesn't say it. I haven't told her that I love her even though I fell in love with her the day she called me to pick her up from the ER.

I peel her from my body and tell her to go to the gallery to keep her mind occupied, and I will stop by on my break. Tears are still falling from her eyes as she nods her head, knowing I am right. She needs to keep herself busy so she doesn't worry too much.

I wipe her tears with my thumb and give her sweet lips a deep kiss. I leave her in bed, hopefully feeling less anxious than she did when she woke up.

I leave her house feeling an emptiness fill my heart. How can I miss her? I haven't even shut the door to my Jeep, and I want to run back inside and hold her for the rest of our lives. I don't know if it is because I am finally happy or because I know life can change in an instant.

Sunny

I watch Luca pull away, and I am still devastated by my dream. He is right. I need to keep myself busy. He promised he would text me and let me know when I could stop by to see him. I can't shake my dream. I keep seeing him hurt, not being able to get out of that house. I don't know where it was, but I was there watching as they tried to get to him. But it is too late. He is gone. My heart no longer exists. That space is filled with nothingness.

When I tell him about the dream, his expression goes from worried to complete relief. There was something else in his eye, but I can't put my finger on what it is. I decide to let the butterflies in my stomach fly free. I am weary from trying to control my emotions after everything that has happened in the past six months. From losing Jake to letting Luca in my world and now falling in love with him, I know how short life is. I will not deny how I feel about Luca anymore. I never want to be without him, and it is time I tell him how I feel.

Lost in my thoughts, I head into the bathroom to get ready to go to the gallery. Ann and I have been swamped between trying to get the rest of the carnival art sent out and planning for the next show. It is scheduled to open in the last week of January. I hate the winter, so I will brighten things up with another saucy show. With lots of colors and encouraging self-love, this show will liven the dreary weather slump most feel that time of year.

My goal has always been to use my talent to help others. Not only am I giving local artists a chance to show themselves off and make some money, but the guests have had a great time every time. Ann has been in touch with the reporters that came out for the last show. Each is putting together a front-page piece featuring The Muse. Things are taking off for us. We have even spoken of hiring a part-time employee to help keep us on track, and it will free up some time for me. Leaving late every night proves to be tiring.

I am brought back to my bathroom when the warm water caresses my skin like a lost love. A lost love: I swear I feel Jake when I am alone. I don't know if I am going crazy, but I hold on to the feeling of him. I miss him more than ever.

At the thought of Jake and the accident, I feel my throat tighten. My stomach turns, and my sight goes dark. I gasp for air, but no matter how deeply I breathe in, my lungs can't get enough. My heart pounds as though it is going to make my chest burst open, and my body is as hot as trees burning in a forest fire. I turn off the hot water and stand freezing under the showerhead. My panic attack slowly starts to dissipate, and my breathing becomes less labored. I am still shaking, but the worst of the attack is over.

I finish up in the shower, and I am walking out the door thirty minutes later. The air is thick as we head into September, and it hasn't rained in weeks, causing the humidity to rise into extremely uncomfortable conditions. I have on a lightweight wrap dress and a pair of ballet flats, which seem to be the most comfortable pieces of clothing I own. I usually kick my shoes off when I get to the gallery anyway—no sense in making my feet hurt for no reason.

Before I push the door to the gallery open, I hear Ann screaming. I can't tell if it is a good or bad scream, so I throw the door open and see the sight of sights. Ann has the gallery phone in one hand while waving her other hand in the air. Not being able to keep her excitement under control, she skips over to me and throws her arms around my neck and kisses my cheek.

"Ann, are you okay?" I tease.

"Sunny, we are more than okay," she squeaks.

"Care to elaborate? I need an Ann-good-news pick-me-up," I share.

She sits at the bar, barely able to keep her butt on the barstool. I take a seat next to her, waiting for the good news. She tells me the rest of the art from the carnival show have been sent out, and thank-you cards have started showing up in the mail. She then rambles about the reporters that had attended as well. Each one had a great time and wrote amazing articles about the gallery. Then she hits me with the big one. We are already sold out for our next show.

I can't believe my ears. "Really?"

I am in shock. We have not started the major work for the show, and we are already sold out.

Just as I stand up to hug her, we hear the sirens of the fire trucks. Ann and I stop, turning to the front window in time to see two of our trucks on their way down the main route going toward the city. Ann grabs my hand and gives me a reassuring squeeze. She coaxes me into sitting down while she calls our breakfast order in.

I just lost my appetite. I feel the color drain from my face, and a hollowness takes me over.

Ann turns on the TV that sits on the counter behind the bar. The sound of the reporter draws my attention even though I stare through her as though only her voice exists.

"We are here live at the corner of Tenth and Elizabeth, where a fire has swallowed four local businesses," she summarizes. "We are told the fire started around nine this morning and started in the bakery before it spread to the deli next door. Local firefighters were on the scene early, but we are told the fire is fast-moving, and reinforcements are coming from surrounding towns."

The screen turns orange with a video of an out-of-control fire with firemen and police all over.

Ann turns to me with a terrified look on her face. I tell her about the dream I had last night. I can feel the heat as if I am burning with him. I smell the smoke as it enters my lungs. I can't breathe, but it isn't me. It's Luca. His large body is limp on the burning floor. No one can get to him.

"Honey, that was a nightmare, not a premonition. Luca will be fine. Can you breathe for me? You haven't taken a single breath since I put the TV on."

"Yeah," I mumble. I force myself to pull air into my body like holding it will help. I continue to watch the news as the video of the roaring fire is played behind the large-breasted brunette. Her red lips move, but I can't make out what she is saying.

The next thing I see is people coming out of the fifth shop in the row. It isn't attached to the others, but it is close enough. A mix of firemen and would-be victims run out as smoke fills the building.

There are a few firemen gathered in front of the fourth shop. They look like they are waiting for something or someone. The next image on the screen turns my blood cold. The reporter speaks with urgency and informs everyone that she is being told the men gathered there are waiting for three firemen to come out. They had gone in looking for a young boy on the third floor.

I am paralyzed with fear when they show a window being broken by someone on the third floor. Two of the men had the boy by the arms and were able to get him to safety. They, on the other hand, were running out of time. They both jump from the third floor. The third fireman was on his way out as the overhang of the building collapsed. The building had been compromised from the fire, and it didn't help that they were old and in desperate need of repair.

I can't tell who the men are. They are covered in debris and are quickly hauled away by EMTs. I look at Ann, but I can't speak. Her eyes are wide, and her mouth hangs open. She turns to me, but before she can say anything, I jump up from the barstool and run to the bathroom. My stomach churns, and thick bile rises in my throat. I start crying. I am unable to stop, and it makes my nose stuffy. I drop to my knees and pull the toilet lid up. Before I know it, I am throwing up—and during a panic attack, no less.

I hear the bathroom door open, but I can't move. Ann tries to comfort me by saying it may not be Luca. It could be the guys from the city's search and rescue, not Luca's squad. I try to calm down and pull myself together. She's right, anyway. I have no idea if it was even Luca's squad.

I stand up with Ann's help and lean against the sink facing the mirror. I turn on the cold water and splash my face, hoping I can calm down. Ann runs upstairs to grab toothpaste and a toothbrush so I can get the rancid taste out of my mouth.

As I come out of the bathroom, Ann helps me back to the bar and calls the diner, telling me I need to eat. About a half hour later, the bell above the front door chimes, and the smell of bacon drifts through the air. We chat with the delivery driver, and as the conversation goes on, my mind stops racing. The man bids us a good day and is on his way. Walking out, he holds the door open for a minute, and I hear him say "good morning" to someone.

I look up, and Mel is standing in front of me with a look that will be burned in my memory forever. Her eyes are sad, and her body language tells more than she is aiming for. She opens her mouth but then closes it as if she is choosing her words with care. Her eyes drop to the floor, and she starts to play with her thumb ring.

"Mel, you are killing me. What the hell is going on? Was that Luca, Ryan, and Jimmy jumping out of a third-story window?"

I am a mess. My mind is going in a thousand directions.

"Yes, it was. Ryan and Jimmy are awake and okay, but Luca got the worst of it. He was in there the longest, and the overhang fell on top of him. I am taking you over. They are at St. Michael's. Let's go," she asserts while grabbing my upper arm.

I turn to Ann, and she shoos Mel and me out the door. She yells to keep her posted.

*****

The ride to the hospital is awful. It feels like the night I got the call about Jake.

This cannot be happening again. This doesn't happen to one person twice, does it?

Pulling into the parking space, Mel turns off the car, and we run inside. The front guard tells us where to go. We head down two hallways and reach the ER double doors. I am not ready for what I see.

Ryan and Jimmy are waiting for us, and they bring us to where Luca is resting. I pull the curtain back and fight the urge to throw up. His head is bandaged, and his left leg is in a cast. When he breathes, it looks like he is in pain.

The doctor that comes by tells me he will be okay, but he is lucky. Luca came away with a broken ankle, a mild concussion, and four broken ribs. The doctor says it could have been much worse.

I pull the rolling stool up to Luca's bed and gently pick up his hand. I rub his fingers between mine, feeling his rough skin calm my nerves.

He squeezes my fingers, forcing my eyes to open. Tears fall effortlessly as he smiles. "I guess your dream had some merit," he jokes.

"I didn't want it to. It scared the shit out of me when I saw you guys head out there. Then Ann turned on the TV, and I felt so helpless." I cry. I can't imagine what I would do if something were to happen to him. Since Luca picked me up after my miscarriage, I have seen a change in him I never thought I would see. He is sweet, caring, and surprisingly, loving. I never wanted him in my life. In fact, I did everything to make sure he wasn't. Now I want him to be by my side for as long as possible.

"They are going to put me in a regular room. The doc wants me to stay the night to monitor me for any breathing or head issues."

"I will stay with you then take you home as soon as they say you can go."

I will take care of him for as long as he needs. Maybe I should hire another person to help Ann and me. Luca is my top priority until he tells me to go back to work.

Just then, a nurse comes in and informs us Luca's bed is ready. They roll him down the hall on a stretcher, the entire time telling the staff he can walk with crutches. I smile knowing he is in no shape to move on his own.

We get to the room, and they get Luca settled in bed. He sighs when they leave, hoping to get some more sleep.

I pull up a thick brown cushion chair next to his bed and lay my head on his right leg. I feel his hand rubbing the back of my head. After a few minutes, I stand up and kiss him as I've never kissed anyone. I am grateful he is okay, and I don't want to lose him, ever.

Luca

Having Sunny with me is refreshing. She cares about me, and today proved how much she cares. It's not like when Sarah would visit if something crazy happened. She would come to make sure I was breathing, and then she was gone. Sunny doesn't want to leave my side. She looks terrified, so I won't tell her what happened. All she needs to know is I am okay. I don't know if they will let her stay the night, but I will find out. She might get upset if they don't let her.

After she gives me a kiss that makes me realize today is the day, Sunny rests her head on my right leg. I rub the back of her head, letting her hair curl around my fingers. I can smell her lavender shampoo through the smell of smoke lingering in my nose. She looks sad and scared, and it breaks my heart.

I just need Ry to stop by my room with the box before he leaves, so I shoot him a text letting him know it is time. Sunny looks up at me, and my heart melts as if every time she looks at me is the first time. Her eyes sparkle, and her skin is radiant even though I can feel her unease.

Sunny's eyelids are too heavy for her to keep open, although she is trying to stay awake. Once she falls asleep on me, I grab my phone and message Ryan that it is time. He messages back with a thumbs-up.

The nurse pops in with another round of mild pain relievers, and I ask if Sunny can stay. She tells me they don't allow anyone after visiting hours, which will end at eight tonight. That gives me three hours with her before she has to leave.

About forty-five minutes later, Ryan walks in with the box I asked him to pick up from my house. I couldn't risk leaving it at Sunny's for her to stumble upon, even if by accident. Ryan hands me the box and asks if I am sure.

"I have never been so sure about anything in my entire life. She feels right, and I am not going to spend the next ten years wondering what if I had just done it," I explain.

He smiles and tells me it is about time I acknowledge how I feel about Sunny—how I have always felt about her. Ryan says "good luck" and leaves me to it.

I can't wait for Sunny to wake up. I am too excited. I have never been too excited about anything in my life, but this is Sunny. I open the box and am still pleased with my choice. I know she will like it. Everything I pick out for her, she loves and looks great in. I take it out of the box and check to make sure she is still sleeping. She is so I carefully sit up, making sure I don't hurt my ribs more than they already hurt. I take her delicate left hand and place the ring on her ring finger. I hope she says yes. The ring is beautiful, just like her. The band is encrusted with diamonds, and the gem is a two-carat center stone.

I lie back down to get comfortable and wait for her to wake up. I am nervous that she won't want this so soon or at all. I won't blame her if she doesn't, especially since our relationship is relatively new, but I want her to be mine. Forever.

With my body stiff and my head feeling like it's ready to explode, I sit up and take Sunny's left hand in mine, turning it face up. The ring I bought her to show how much I love her is resting beside me. I gently start tracing circles in the palm of her hand. She takes a deep sleepy breath and opens her unfocused eyes. Her smile grows as she becomes fully aware of what I am doing.

"Hey, good girl. Welcome back."

"Hey." She yawns as she straightens. "How are you feeling?"

"As long as you are here, I am perfect," I assure her.

"What are you doing?" she probes.

"I want to tell you a story," I explain. "There once was a boy who was secretly in love with a girl. The way her eyes sparkled when she smiled made his heart stop. The boy had a hard time hiding his attraction to a girl he had no business being with. She was the opposite of what type of girl he was expected to date, and this turned his heart to ice. He went to great lengths to ensure her hatred for him. Little did she know how he longed to be with her.

"Many years later, the boy and the girl were brought together by a chance tragedy, changing their lives forever. The boy carried a tremendous amount of guilt for how he treated the girl and for the tragedy he brought upon them both. After months of trying to apologize for all the hurt he caused her, she finally let her walls down to let him help her. He tried his best, but she still didn't trust him. He gave her space, but one night, he couldn't take it anymore and decided to come clean about his part in their tragedy. He went to her and confessed everything to her. Instead of screaming at him, she comforted him. He couldn't keep his love for her a secret any longer. He tried to resist his feelings, but the time was now. He decided to take her where she stood, and with no argument, she let him. Since that night, he knew he never wanted to be without her. Sunny, I never want to be without you."

I turn her hand over so she can see the ring I placed on her finger. "We both know life is short, nothing is forever, and tomorrow is never a promise. Would you do me the immense honor of being my beautiful wife?"

Her mouth drops open, and her eyes fill with tears that quickly run down her cheeks. "Yes. Yes, of course, I will be your wife. Luca, I love you more than you know."

Sunny jumps from her seat and throws her arms around my neck. I feel her tears on my face as her lips crash into mine. She pulls away and stares into my eyes as though she is trying to savor this exact moment.

"You okay, my good girl?"

"Yeah. I just never thought you and I would be here, like this. I thought I would never love anyone again after the accident. Here you are, never giving up on trying to tell me how you feel, and me feeling the same way," she submits.

I put my arm around her waist and pull her close so I can devour her sweet lips one more time before visiting hours are over. She is sad she can't stay, but she promised everything would be ready at home for when the hospital releases me tomorrow.

I give her the keys to my house, which Ryan brought in with the ring. I have a rancher, so it will be easier for me to get around and not have to rely on Sunny too much. She kisses me one more time then hurries off to meet Ryan and Mel downstairs.

Feeling elated, I watch TV before I finally fall asleep.

Sunny

I get to Luca's around 10:00 p.m. I stopped at the grocery store, knowing that Luca had no food in his house because he has been staying with me. We briefly talked about selling both homes and buying something that is ours. Holding a few bags of groceries, I have a small battle with one of the locks on the front door. Eventually, the lock turns, and I kick the door the rest of the way open. Yanking my keys from the lock, I hope I do not drop the heavy bags as they start to slip from my arms. I am still on the phone with Mel as I fumble to find the switch on the wall. Raising my arms with a strategic effort, I manage to flip on the living room light. I freeze.

What the hell is going on?

I drop the groceries with no control over what my body is doing. The eggs break on the floor, and cold milk spills over my feet, but I don't dare move. I can only focus on the light bouncing off the shiny metal. Angela, from my doctor's office, is sitting in Luca's recliner with a gun pointed my way. He mentioned before that he had taken her out once but that she became clingy, on the verge of stalking him. He assured me this was taken care of. It has not been taken care of.

"Sunny? Are you okay? What is going on?" I hear a panicked Mel screaming through the phone.

"Angela. Hi, how are you?" My voice trembles.

"Cut the shit, Sunny. Where is Luca?" she asks. Her facial expression is blank and doesn't change. Her sweet voice is deep and monotone. Her eyes pierce my skin like an ice-cold blade. She sits cross-legged with her gun pointed at my head. "Pick up your phone and hand it over," she demands.

Slowly, I bend down to lose connection with the outside world and end the call with Mel. I inform her the hospital is keeping him overnight for observation. "Do you know what happened to him today, Angela?"

"I heard. When is he coming back?"

"Angela, I know you may think you have feelings for him, but you only went out once. He told me everything about that night. How much do you *really* know him, sweetheart?" I try to get her to talk to me.

"Do you know what he did to me? Do you know how he treated me?" She screams, jumping out of the chair. Her hand shakes, but she is still pointing her gun at me.

"No, Angela, I don't. Why don't you tell me about it?" I plead with her, trying to figure out what to do. I have my cell phone in my back pocket, but I don't want her to do anything stupid.

"Sit down and slide your phone to me," she instructs.

Luca still has a landline in the kitchen. I'll see if I can get her anything. "Okay. Do you want something to drink?"

"Does he have beer?"

"Of course, he has beer. I'll get you one." I walk to the kitchen, pretending I am not terrified. *What the hell did he do to her?* I carefully pick up the phone and dial 9-1-1.

"9-1-1, what's your emergency?"

"I'm at my fiancé's house, and there is a young woman here with a gun," I whisper.

"Okay, ma'am. Where is the address you are at?"

"It's 415 Marvin Drive in Arden Manor," I answer.

"Do you know the woman holding the gun?"

"Yes. Her name is Angela Harmon. Please hurry," I beg.

At that, I can hear Angela calling for me, wondering where I am. I drop the phone on the counter, not hanging up so the dispatcher can keep an ear on the situation. I take a deep breath and grab her a beer from the fridge.

When I get back to the living room, I can see Angela's body is rigid. Her knuckles are white as she grips the gun. Her jaw is clenched, and her eyes are puffy as she looks at me with disdain. Handing her the beer, I sit down on the sofa across from her.

"Angela, you are a sweet girl. What are you doing here? With a gun? This is not who you are," I remind her.

"I was a sweet girl until he made me realize how little I mean to people. Especially men. Do you know what he did, Sunny?"

"No, honey, I don't. Why don't you tell me?" I answer.

"He loves you. You wouldn't understand. He used me. He won't do that to you. He won't hurt you. Why was it okay for him to do it to me?" She weeps. Her eyes are full of tears, and they drop before she has a chance to wipe them away. She sniffles, wiping her nose on the black sleeve of her free hand.

"You know, Luca and I did not get along for a long time. Angela, talk to me. Please," I beg.

"My friend told me that his wife died and that he was lonely. He liked the younger women, and he told my friend he thought I was cute." Sniffling, she continues, "I told my friend to have him call me."

She stops and looks out the window then back at me. "We ended up going to a nice restaurant. Then he brought me back here. I let him have sex with me. He almost fucking tore me in half." Her eyes drop to the floor, the tears still flowing. "Then when he was done with me, he called me a fucking cab," she shrieks. "Not to mention, that night, he got me pregnant, and I didn't know what to do. I didn't make up my mind as to what I should do. Not until I saw him bring you to the doctor's office after your miscarriage. The way he looked at you and the fact that he stood so close as if he would brutally murder anyone who tried to hurt you, I knew he would never do that for me. That was the day I decided to have an abortion."

My heart sank to the floor as she told me her story. I have nothing. She caught me. "Oh, Angela. I am so sorry that happened to you. No one deserves to be treated like that. When we were younger, Luca and I did not like each other. He made fun of me constantly and made me feel worthless. Kind of like he made you feel worthless."

"So why are you here, at his house? Why are you wearing what I assume is a ring he gave you? Sunny, it doesn't make sense."

"No, Angela. It doesn't. When I found out why Luca treated me the way he did, things made more sense, and my wounds healed a little bit. Sometimes knowing why a person does something can help you move on. He just lost Sarah. He was drinking a lot, and his reputation somehow got worse. Why would you want to date him?"

"He is what I want. He is handsome, fun, has a great job, and he paid attention to me. I want that in my life constantly. Not just when it is convenient for him or any other guy."

"Look, I am not in any way excusing him for the way he treated you. He had a wound that he never thought would heal. And trust me, he still has a long way to go. He was in a dark place. Unfortunately, you happened to be on his road of destruction." I stop and study her eyes. She is lost in what I am telling her. "Please, Angela. Find a way to forgive him. And yourself."

"Why would I need to forgive myself?"

"Because you think it is your fault he treated you like this, but it is not. Not by a long shot. When people are broken, they do mean and cold things to others. You will find out it happens more often than you think." I shift in my chair, hearing the police siren in the distance. My body starts to relax. "Do yourself a favor. Learn from this. Do not ever let another man treat you like that. Be smart about what you give someone and how soon you give it to them."

The living room is lit with the flashing red lights from the police cruisers as sirens fill the empty night. Angela looks around but realizes she has nowhere to run. I hear pounding on the door, and someone yells, "Rolling Hills PD. Open up."

My heart is beating out of my chest, and tears stream down my face, both from fear and relief. Angela is frozen where she sits but says nothing, and the gun is still pointed at me. The police bang on the door again, and yet Angela still does not move.

My stomach churns as I think about how I may never see Luca again. Sweat runs slowly down my neck as I watch Angela get more and more nervous. "Angela, just open the door. They are going to come in either way," I plead.

Angela stands and peeks out of the side window to see what she is up against. When she looks back at me, her face is clear of feelings. Her eyes turn to stone as they capture me in fear. This is a bad situation.

"Don't you see?" she challenges me. "Luca is going to shatter your heart. He treats women like they are made for him to play with and throw away. That noose you call an engagement ring is just so you can't just leave when he finally breaks you."

"What makes you think he wants to break me? Or that I would let him break me?" I sass.

"Sunny, who do you think are you kidding? Everyone knows your little 'love story,'" Angela mocks. "Boy destroys girl when they are young. Girl never fully recovers. Boy weasels his way back into girl's life and destroys her again. The only difference is now the girl has a much harder time trying to get away from the boy because now they are married. Get it?" Her eyes dart to the front door. She is quiet, pointing her gun at me.

"Please," I plead. "Don't do this, Angela. Your life will be over."

"My life has been over for a long time," she admits.

Another loud knock on the front door halts our conversation. "Angela Harmon, we know you are in there. We also know there is someone else in there with you. Is everyone okay?" the officer asks.

"We are fine," Angela screams back. "Go away. I am trying to help my friend see she is making a horrible mistake."

"Angela, maybe we can help her together. Can you let me in?" answers a sweet voice.

"Who is that? Who are you? You can't help me explain this to her," Angela barks back.

"My name is Officer O'Hara. Is this about Luca Claymont? I heard about that guy," she replies. "I know men like him, always out to hurt a woman. Especially young and sweet women like you. How about I come in and talk to you both? Is that okay?"

Angela walks to the door and rests her forehead against it as she decides if she will give in and open the door or if she will keep the charade going a little longer. At this point, I am not as scared as I was, but this needs to end. My nerves are shot, and all I want is for Luca to be home and Angela in a jail cell.

The sound of Angela releasing the lock on the front door is music to my ears. Officer O'Hara asks Angela to put the gun on the floor and open the door. Surprisingly, Angela does as she is told.

Once the gun is on the floor, Angela opens the door and takes a few steps back. Before I know it, Officer O'Hara is inside cuffing a sobbing Angela. I sit in the chair, unable to move. Until I hear him.

I jump out of the chair, and there is Luca. Ryan is on one side of him and Mel on the other, helping him inside. Luca's presence makes me feel safe, even though he is a bit broken at the moment. I walk over and take Mel's place at his side, helping him to the couch.

"Are you all right, my good girl?" he asks. His eyes are fixed on mine, and his hand is caressing my cheek.

"I am now. I don't know how she got in. She was here when I got back from the store after I left the hospital. I think you should press charges."

"I will. But are you sure you are okay?" he presses.

"Yes," I reply, rubbing my temples. I drop onto the couch next to him.

Putting his arm around me, he pulls me close enough to kiss me, but he doesn't. Instead, he whispers in my ear that he wants to start a family.

"Tonight?" I laugh.

"Right now, right here."

"Can we wait until everyone clears out?" I giggle.

"I suppose." He laughs.

Epilogue: Nine Months Later

Sunny

"Come on, my good girl. Just breathe. Try to take deeper breaths. I promise you will be okay," he encourages.

I can feel every bit of pain as the Jeep picks up speed, racing down the winding pavement. Luca grabs my hand, keeping his eyes on the slick road. It's summer and the rain falls hard, making it difficult to see. This causes my heart to race and leaves my mind in a spiraling panic. One second and things can change; he is going too fast.

I feel him squeeze my hand. "Good girl. Please breathe," he pleads.

Closing my eyes, I let my breath go and listen to him because the pain is getting worse, and I feel faint. I start feeling nauseous, and my mouth is dry.

"I can't believe I let you talk me into coming out here," I whisper between breaths. I am utterly terrified. "We won't make it in time." The tears flow down my cheeks, mixing with the sweat pouring out of my body. "Luca, what if we don't make it? I'm scared."

Luca smiles. "You act as if I've never delivered a baby before."

"You did? When?"

"For my cousin. A few years ago. A few of us went to a campground, an hour from where she lived at the time. She wasn't due for a few weeks, so we thought she would be fine. Little did we know my nephew was ready to come out the day after we got there. She went into labor, and before we could get to the hospital, he was on his way. Nothing we could do but deliver him then and there. Don't worry, my good girl. I will take care of you. As long as I'm around, you have nothing to worry about. I got you."

"I had no idea you did that. It's amazing. You are amazing." I sit back in the seat with some relief knowing Luca is here with me. I squeeze his hand as another contraction takes over my body. I practice my breathing, and being the wonderful man he is, Luca is breathing with me.

"Luca, the baby is coming now. We won't make it to the hospital. Please pull over."

"Okay, good girl. Just hang on. We can do this," he assures me.

We pull over on the side of the quiet road. Luca opens the door and helps me out so I can lie down in the back seat. I'm so glad he traded in his old Jeep for the new four-door one, or this would be near impossible. The rain slows a little, but the thunder is loud, calming my nerves. Just as Luca finishes putting the blanket on the seat and I lie back, my contractions are close together, and it is time.

Luca coaches me through breathing, pushing, then more breathing and more pushing. What feels like hours of pain is over the second I hear our baby cry. A loud and healthy cry. Luca wraps our little one in a blanket as I sit up. I look at them, baby and daddy, with a warmth in my heart I never thought I would have.

Luca hands me our bundle. "Mommy, meet your daughter."

I am so relieved when I see her angelic face. I look at Luca, and he sits next to me in the back seat with his arm around my shoulders, holding me as tight as he can. "Okay, can we get to a hospital? I want to make sure she's perfect."

"She came from you. She's more than perfect," he responds, kissing my cheek softly. "But yes, we need to get everyone checked out. What do you want to name her?" he asks.

"How about Iris? In Greek, it translates to 'rainbow.' And in Greek mythology, Iris was the goddess of the rainbow."

"Why do you want to name her after a rainbow?"

"Because she is our rainbow—the beauty left behind after the storm passes. And there is a huge one right in front of us."

Luca looks up. "Well, I'll be. Iris it is. Ready to hit the road with our little family, my love?"

"Yes. Let's get out of here and get checked out," I agree.

The End